The Watchmaker
Part One

B.L. Blocher

The Emerald City Press— Southington, CT
ISBN: 978-0-578-65204-7
Library of Congress Control Number: 2020903609
Title: *The Watchmaker, Part One*
Author: B.L. Blocher
Digital distribution | 2020
Paperback | 2020

Thewatchmaker1939@gmail.com

Dedication

I dedicate this book to my mother Rachela and my father Jurek. Both Holocaust survivors, I used true fragments of their experiences and intertwined them into this fictional story. Surviving for them however, didn't quite mean they were mentally unscathed or that they could lead a normal life.

INTRODUCTION

I was frequently awakened by my mother screaming in the middle of the night as she was experiencing horrific dreams of her time during the Holocaust in Poland. I can honestly say that she never had a "good" dream, where she woke up the following morning and talked about anything beautiful and happy. They were always nightmarish and involved being chased, caught or some other heinous atrocity involving the Nazis.

I also had the daunting task of routinely being trapped in the car with her as she revealed all sorts of incomprehensible and tragic stories from her time in the concentration camps. I only say "Trapped" because the stories were difficult to comprehend and in such detail as I was only a little boy. I never knew what to say, mostly because I was choking down my emotions so she wouldn't see me upset. I always felt my mom had it worse than my father though. She was in the camps. Starving, sick, desperately trying to survive. She was forced to take ice cold showers in the gas chamber room.

Never knowing if water or gas was going to come out of the shower heads.

My father on the other hand was very introverted about his time during the war. He didn't talk much about it. Maybe that's why I felt my mother had it worse.

What we knew was that he managed to escape from the ghetto and hid in a swamp for several days. He made his way by night to a friend's farm. Konstantyn Dabrowski, an admirable Polish farmer and his family who took him in and hid him in the hayloft of their barn.

After some time there, a neighbor became suspicious and my father had to leave. He then found his way, sick and freezing to the Joachim Iluk family farm. Joachim, his daughter Felicja and her fifteen year old son Henryk, were another noble and compassionate Polish family, who took my father in and cared for him. Hiding him for the duration of the war. Both families contributed heroically to save my father's life. It was a tremendous risk for both farmers. If he was discovered by the Germans or Polish bounty hunters on their farms, the Germans would have slaughtered the farmers and their entire families for harboring a Jew.

For this risk both families are registered in Israel at the Yad Vashem's database as: "Righteous among the Nations". A prestigious compilation of commended courageous Polish families, that helped save Jews lives during the Holocaust, who emphatically risked their own lives in the event if they were caught.

We later discovered, after my father's death, that he actually had another family before us in Poland. A wife, Zlota and two small children. Katriel his 5 year old little boy, and Sarah his 2 year old little girl. They were only babies, yet the German assassins had no compassion or empathy for even children. They were all savagely murdered by the Nazi's and their collaborators.

Now, because of a DNA genealogy search, we became aware that my father had another son, with Felicja Soroko (Joachim Iluks adult daughter). His name was Kazimierz. Sadly he died in 2004 in Poland. Unfortunately, my father never spoke of his past family members. It's a mystery why he didn't. I often wondered what he was thinking about when he sat in his chair in a trance, watching me as I played, hardly ever engaging with me. Not that he wasn't loving towards me, it's just certain things were off limits.

Now that I have children, I can understand what he must have felt. He must have been extremely sad inside, thinking about his other little children and missing them.

I wrote this story out of fantasy.

"How can I go back in time, and get retribution on those heartless Nazi monsters that hurt my family, the children and the millions of other people they murdered?"

The only way possible... in my mind, on paper, and with a Watchmaker and his lethal children.

Chapter One

As I sit in my classroom I stare intently at the clock.

My Torah instructor rambles on about the goodness of charity, especially when it comes to giving to the synagogue. The second-hand ticks precisely, as each rotation draws me nearer to the long day's end. If I watch closely enough I can even see the minute hand, ever so slowly make its way to the next minute mark. I am fascinated by clocks. How we are all constrained by time and its effects. Regardless of circumstance, time marches on. There is nothing we can do about it. We must obey time or pay the consequences. Time is in my blood. My heart does not beat. Rather it ticks like a clock.

After all, my great grandfather was a "*Zeiger Meister*," a famous watch master who once made a pocket watch for the King of Prussia. He taught his son—my grandfather-- to be a *Zeiger Meister*. He in turn trained my father Joseph to continue the art. Someday it will be my turn, but for now I am only allowed to sweep the floor and wind up the 100 clocks that are displayed in our store.

My family's watch shop has been on the same street corner in the city of Vilna, Poland since 1875. It was named Imperial Watch and Clock by my great grandfather, but the anti-Semitic locals would just refer to it as the Jew Screw. We were "The Jews." Many of my father's customers were too.

There was a constant flow of Jewish patrons in and out of the store. But many non-Jews also came, since there were no other repair shops that could fix most anything. Sometimes my father was called upon to repair odd things such as false teeth and eyeglass frames.

"If you are a *Zeiger Meister* you can fix anything," he used to brag.

It was a lucrative business. We were better off than most of the residents of Vilna, but we were modest in the way we displayed our wealth. My father was a generous man, especially when it came to helping the poor and needy.

I can remember an incident about three years ago, in the winter of 1938. I was helping my father on a cold blustery Friday afternoon. We were preparing to close the shop for Sabbath, when the door swung open. A burst of ice-cold air swept into the store, causing the bell on the door to fall off. A middle-aged man, who was poorly dressed, bent over to pick it up. He was holding a small tin pail.

"I'm so sorry," he said in Polish.

Instantly we knew he was not a Jew, since a Jew would have spoken our language, Yiddish. My father came from the back room, removed his jeweler's loupe, which was always attached to his head by a wire, and wiped his hands on a towel. The man stood there, looking around the store in amazement. The store instantly became overwhelmed with the foul stench of animal excrement which emitted from the man's clothing.

"You have so many clocks!" he marveled. "And each one has exactly the correct time!"

"You should be here when the hour strikes and hear the racket it makes!" joked my father.

Even though it was obvious the man was poor and smelled horrible, my father treated him with utmost respect.

"Are you interested in a clock, sir?" my father asked.

The man took off his hat and looked down at the floor.

"My name is Dombrovsky. I am a poor farmer from Michalishek. It is a small town about 20 kilometers south from here," he stated.

"A farmer, that would explain the stench," I thought. "I have three daughters and a wife who is sick. I came to town to trade some butter so I can buy shoes for my girls. They have nothing to wear on their feet. I went to the shoe store, but the Jew shoe maker refused to trade with me. I asked many strangers to buy my butter, but no one would. I stood on the sidewalk and begged for money, but no one would help me. A policeman asked me what I was doing. I told him I came to town to trade my butter for shoes, but I had no luck. The policeman suggested, 'Why don't you go see the Jew in the Jew Screw over there? He has lots of money. Maybe he needs some butter!' I had nothing to lose, so I decided to ask you," he continued.

My father cringed when he heard the term "Jew Screw," but chalked it up to ignorance.

"I also have children, my friend," my father responded. "I have a nine-year-old son Jacob over there—we call him Koby-- and a little girl Hanna, who is three. She is at home with my wife, preparing for the Sabbath."

The man glanced down at my feet, to see what kind of shoes I was wearing.

My father invited the man to sit down as he laid the towel he was holding across the glass case, which housed a very expensive collection

4

of watches. My father left him standing there and returned with two short glasses, a bottle of liquor and a loaf of bread.

"You look like you could use a Schnaps," my father joked as he poured the liquor into the glasses.

The man moved closer. My father remarked that indeed we were out of butter. He began slicing the loaf of bread. Dombrovsky watched as my father dipped his knife into the tin. Most of the butter was frozen solid, but he managed to scrape off enough of it to spread on three pieces of bread. My father handed me a piece. The butter appeared crusty and filthy.

"Before I buy anything, I have to sample it" stated my father.

My father looked at me and with his stern eyes. That told me I had better at least pretend to eat the bread so as not to embarrass the man. We apprehensively took a bite.

"Hmmm...this is very good butter. Your milk cow must be special. How much do you want for it?" asked my father.

I stood motionless as I watched my father begin to "haggle" with the man.

"What do you think is a fair price?" the man said tentatively.

"Koby, how much should I pay for this butter?" father asked. He surprised me with that question. I had always been taught to be quiet, and not interfere.

All I could do was shrug my shoulders and make a silly face. My father turned to the man, clasping his hands together.

"OK, the last time I bought butter I paid one zlote. I will give you one zlote."

The man seemed to be deeply disappointed with that amount. Shoes would be much more than that. My father reached into his pocket and handed over the coin.

The man nodded his head, took the money and thanked my father for the drink and bread. Then he headed for the door.

"Hey, Dombrovsky come back here! I forgot something!" my father shouted.

Dombrovsky turned back towards my father. "What did you forget, sir?" he asked.

My father replied, "I paid you for the butter, but I didn't pay for the metal tin it was in!" Thereupon he handed Dombrovsky an envelope which contained fifty zlote in it!

Dombrovsky was stunned! It was a fortune to him. He began to quiver.

"How is it that you are doing this for me? I am a stranger to you, a nobody!"

My father put his hand on the man's shoulder. "Did we not share a Schnaps together? I only drink with my friends," said my father.

Dombrovsky began to cry, thanking my father over and over again.

Finally my father told the man he had better get going before the shoe store closed. The man shook my father's hand and left the shop. I was astonished to have witnessed the entire encounter.

"What do you think about this Jacob?" my father asked.

"I knew something was going on in your head the way you were carrying on," I replied.

"I felt sorry for him. But to be honest, I wanted to test him."

"What sort of test, Papa? All you did was have a drink with him and you bought his butter?"

"It was about the one zlote for the butter. He was content to get anything. He appreciated even one zlote. I had a good feeling about him. Maybe someday he will return the favor."

I shrugged my shoulders and made a silly face again. "Maybe" I said.

***

Fridays are always a hectic day for Jews.

The Sabbath begins on Friday at sundown and lasts until sundown on Saturday.

In winter sundown comes quite early. If you aren't prepared, it could be a challenge.

I always wondered what would happen if someone actually stayed out too late. My father believes that women helped influence this commandment to put the fear of God in their husbands to get them home in time for supper, while the Sabbath meal was still hot.

I left school in a hurry. It was Friday afternoon and I had to help my father close the store.

Running as fast as I could, I barged in, almost knocking the bell off the door. My father, who was finishing a watch, glanced up at me.

"Go pull down the metal fence over the storefront and lock the front door. We have to be home before sunset. Then take the watches out of the display case and put them in the safe."

I locked up the store and turned the sign from "Open" to "Closed." Then I went behind the display case. There was a blue velvet tray underneath, which we used to collect the watches.

One by one I picked up each watch and gently placed in onto the velvet tray.

I was careful as I walked through the door towards the safe. If I dropped a watch, it could be costly. I pulled the safe door open and placed the tray on a shelf within the vault.

While the door was open, I couldn't help but notice all the valuable things stored in it. In one of the drawers there was a watch that was special and not for sale. It was created by my grandfather. He made it for me when I was born. He said it was to be my Bar Mitzvah gift, when I turned thirteen.

Next year it will be mine! It was a magnificent piece, which had a round dial with an automatic winder built inside. The bracelet was a combination of 18 karat red, yellow and white gold in a zig-zag pattern.

The 18k yellow gold watch case was surrounded by diamonds and a golden see-through dial. The numbers were also made of diamonds except for the number 12, which was a bright red ruby.

My concentration was broken by a knock at the back door. It was my grandfather.

"My children come on. The sun is going down. We have to get home, or our wives will report us to God!" he chuckled. He saw me holding The Watch and he came up behind me.

"Jacob," he said, "I made this watch so you will always remember all the love I have for you." I smiled as he put his arms around me and hugged me from behind.

"I engraved something special inside on the case for you to see when you are older," he said.

"I know, *Zaydee,* you told me a thousand times!" I chuckled.

We finished closing the shop. As I turned off the lights, all the clocks began to chime. It was 4 o'clock. The Sabbath had begun.

My grandfather hurried out the back door with us. As he turned to close the door, he slipped on the ice and fell down on his arm.

We quickly helped him up but unfortunately his wrist was sprained. It seemed he would be out of commission for a few weeks.

"You know what the women are going to say. God was angry with me for being late and he put ice down under my feet!!" exclaimed grandfather.

"Let's get going before he makes us all fall down!" I laughed.

***

By the following Monday my grandfather's wrist was swollen and sore. It was impossible for him to work on watches. My father insisted he stay at home and rest.

Since my school was nearby, I walked with my father to the shop every day. As we approached the store we noticed a short, skinny young man waiting by the front door. He had a small briefcase in his hand, and he was hopping up and down to stay warm.

My father fumbled with the keys. He asked the man if he didn't mind waiting a few minutes while we prepared to open the store.

He nodded as he watched us walk around the corner to access the back door.

As the store was heating up, and I took items out of the safe, I kept noticing the man outside, still hopping up and down to stay warm.

"Papa, we better let that man in before he freezes to death out there!" I joked.

My father quickly opened the door and lifted the steel fence that secured our shop. "It sure is a cold one today!" my father said, as he let the man in.

"What can I do for you, my friend?"

The young frail man took off his hat, displaying perfectly parted blond hair and piercing blue eyes.

"I am from Germany. My name is Wolfgang, but my friends call me Wolfie. I'm a graduate of the Berlin school of *Zeiger Meisters*. Times are hard. I could not find work in my country, so I am looking for work here. Could you use some help around your shop?" he asked.

"Well that depends" answered my father. "It just so happens I am short- handed this week. How do you feel about working for a Jew?"

"Well as long as you don't try to circumcise me, I'm okay with it!" he replied.

"Well, first I have to see what you can do. My experience with the Berlin school of watchmakers has been disappointing."

"Here is a broken watch. Let me see if you can fix it. If you can get it working, I'll give you a job. If you can't, I'll start you as an apprentice and teach you the right way to repair watches. But you must agree to teach me how to speak your language. Agreed?" asked my father.

"Agreed," replied the young man.

My father made a place for him at one of the worktables. Wolfie opened up his briefcase and removed his tools. I walked over to watch him as he began nervously taking apart the watch.

"I'm Jacob, but you can call me Koby," I said.

Oddly, he seemed to ignore me, as he nervously fumbled with his tools.

I was late for school and my father reminded me to get going. Reluctantly I left and ran off. When I arrived at the school, there was a tumult in the building. Teachers were all up in arms over rumors that the German army was preparing to invade Poland this summer.

I thought it would be better to leave the shouting of the teachers and go to the bathroom, where at least it would be quieter.

There, I found my best friend Benny cleaning up in the sink. He was washing dried animal blood off his hands and arms. I recognized him immediately from his yarmulke, which he never took off. It was deep royal blue and embroidered with a large sparkling silver Star of David in the center.

His family was very religious. It was typical for men in his family to wear yarmulkes all the time. Benny's father was a *shechet*, a rabbi with the authority to slaughter animals.

In order for the dietary laws of Jews to be upheld, all meats must be certified kosher by him. The *shechet* has only one task--to bless and kill the animal by slitting its throat with a blade and letting its blood drain out. The rest is up to the butcher.

The shechet uses a special knife called a *chalaf*. It consists of a thin flat blade about 2" wide and is approximately 18" long. The top of the blade runs straight into a three-quarter-inch wooden or ivory handle. The bottom of the blade, the business side, is honed to a razor-sharp edge as so the animal should not sense any pain from the lethal stroke.

The *chalaf* has no point. It just ends squarely like a ruler. It is not designed to stab or chop. Its only purpose is to painlessly slice open the throats of animals.

According to Judaic law, cutting the animal's throat, if done properly, is deemed painless and humane. However to be kosher, the throat must be sliced with one continuous stroke and pass cleanly through the animal's esophagus and trachea. Otherwise it cannot be certified Kosher and not fit for consumption.

That law must have been conceived way before guns were invented, back when they would have probably clubbed their animals to death. I didn't see much humanity in it, cutting an animal's throat and watching it thrash about with its head barely attached and blood spurting everywhere doesn't seem very friendly to me.

Benny's father would handle the large cows and Benny would process smaller animals such as goats and chickens. I personally didn't have the stomach for it. The only time I ever tagged along with them, I couldn't eat meat for a month!

"How many innocent baby animals did you kill today?" I joked.

"All of them! Short and sharp!" Benny replied. Besides this gory job Benny had, he was quite a character. He was unusually tall and muscular for his age of fifteen. He looked more like a young man than a teenager. He was a comedian and he also had a sarcastic streak. Sometimes bordering on the obnoxious-- especially if someone was unkind to him or a friend, he couldn't let it go.

"Hey, everyone is talking about the German invasion" I said.

"It's impossible! The polish army will crush those barbarians!" Benny exclaimed.

I hoped he was right.

***

The day dragged on. I was eager to return to my father's shop to see how Wolfie had done with that broken watch.

I told Benny about Wolfie and he wanted to come with me after school to meet him. I think he wanted to see what a German looked like since he had never seen one before.

I told him he could come, but only if he promised not to talk to him. I knew if Wolfie would have ignored him as he had done to me earlier that day, Benny wouldn't let it go.

When the final bell rang, we raced out the door and headed for the shop. Benny and I ran as fast as we could, bumping into people along the way. When we finally reached the store, we burst in, knocking the bell off the door. A loud crashing clang interrupted the silence. My father and Wolfie looked up to see what the racket was.

"So? Did he fix the watch?" I questioned my father.

"Not exactly. He is more of a shoemaker than a watchmaker, but I offered to teach him, with a little pay, and he agreed. And he is going to tutor me in German," said my father.

Benny wandered over to Wolfie's workbench and stared at him.

I held my breath, when I noticed Benny trying to hold back from talking to Wolfie.

"Benny, let's go get some candy from the candy shop!" I said. But Benny wasn't paying attention. He began to zero in and speak to Wolfie. "So you're from Germany?" Benny asked.

Wolfie ignored him, just as he had done to me earlier that day. Benny was taken aback by Wolfie's attitude. He was determined to get some form of response from him. "Benny, come with me, let's go get a snack!" I pleaded. I was desperately trying to derail him.

"What's the story with sauerkraut?" chuckled Benny. Nothing from Wolfie.

"Benny, please!!" I begged.

Finally he glanced at me and winked! Oh no Benny, don't do it, I thought to myself! I knew what that look meant. The next question was going to be the game changer.

"So, Wolfie, do you piss like a dog with one leg lifted off the floor or do you squat like your dog bitch mother?" taunted Benny.

Wolfie became enraged and lunged for him! His teeth clenched, his bright red face contorted, and anger filled his fists.

Benny was quick enough to seek refuge behind my father, who had just walked back into the repair area.

Wolfie quickly returned to his chair. My dad asked what was going on.

"Just getting acquainted with Mr. Wolfie," Benny smirked. As my father turned away, Wolfie ran his finger across his throat.

I had a feeling that something was very bad about Wolfie, and we better stay clear of him.

The relationship worsened over time as Benny continued to aggravate and taunt Wolfie.

I worried what might happen if one day my father wasn't there to protect Benny. One thing for sure, Wolfie had his sights set on him.

One afternoon, as we were closing shop and putting the watches in the safe, my grandfather opened up the drawer where my special watch was kept.

"I want to show this to Wolfie," he said.

I followed behind him as he showed him the watch. Wolfie's eyes lit up. He asked if he could hold it.

My grandfather obliged, carefully handing it over. Wolfie stared at the dial and laid the watch on his wrist. As I watched him admiring my Watch, I had an uneasy feeling...

My grandfather told him how he made the watch for me when I was a baby.

Wolfie continued to study the watch and feel its heft. It was obvious that he was intrigued by it. He reluctantly handed it back to my grandfather who then returned it back to the safe and placed it back in the small drawer.

I noticed Wolfie was intently watching where my grandfather was putting it. I was relieved when the safe was finally closed.

Chapter Two

Our good fortune was coming to an end.

The Germans, as feared, did invade Poland that summer of 1939. Wolfie had suddenly disappeared, no thanks or goodbyes.

By the spring of 1941 we were placed under martial law. All the Jews were assigned yellow cloth stars to wear on our sleeves. The Germans were ordering all the Jews to leave their homes and report to fenced-in barbed wire ghettos that they established on the edge of town.

Our Polish neighbors, who were once our friends and customers, were now confiscating all our furniture, clothing and personal possessions. They were treating us terribly: Spitting at us as we walked down the street and sometimes throwing rocks followed by derogatory words. It had become extremely unsafe for us.

It was early autumn. My family and grandparents took refuge in the basement of our watch shop. We lived in a tiny secret room that my father had built in case of an emergency. It was designed to blend in with the plaster walls and no one knew of it. There was a small safe and enough food and water to last for some time. We even had electricity with a small radio and light. When the door was closed, it looked like part of the wall. It was the perfect hiding place. My father had permanently drawn down the metal fence that protected the store and dead bolted the front and back doors. Even if someone could break in, they would never find us. So we thought.

We stayed hidden in our room for several weeks until one rainy night. The wind howled and the water poured down from the sky. We heard a gang of men shouting and banging on the steel fence that protected the shop's windows.

My father went upstairs to see what was going on. There were several German SS soldiers banging on the front door with a battering ram. It was the Gestapo, Hitler's special police. They were feared by everyone including the regular German army, since they had ultimate power and their own agenda.

We heard the bell clang over the door at each hit and finally it fell to the floor as they broke the lock and forced their way in. The lead officer seemed to know his way about the store. My father, hearing all the commotion, told us to stay quiet as we hid in our secret room and he locked the door from the inside.

I could hear my father's watch ticking on his wrist as we held our breaths. Tick. Tick. Tick. Tick. Tick. Tick ...

Within a few seconds we heard them storming down the stairs with their savage dogs barking ferociously outside of our door. They quickly found our secret room and they smashed in the door.

The SS soldiers brutally dragged us out of the room shouting at us in German while beating us with their guns.

We stood there trembling. Then a short Gestapo officer wearing a black uniform, tall black boots, a long black trench coat and a perfectly formed hat carefully came down the feeble staircase.

I noticed he had a large bloody bandage on the side of his neck, as he approached.

"They are here, Major!" an officer shouted as he revealed to him our hiding place.

The Major walked into our safe room and began tossing about our things as if he was looking for something.

As he marched out of the room, I suddenly realized that he looked familiar. Those piercing blue eyes could only belong to one person.

It was Wolfie! I felt a bit of relief, hoping that since my father helped him when he was down and out, that he was here to help us.

He approached my father, stopped, tilted his head and hit him across the face with his pistol, knocking him to the floor.

A tick, tick, ticking sound went off in my head. It pulsed like a heartbeat as I saw my father lying there. His watch crystal had shattered when he hit the floor. The sound in my head became louder and louder!

"Open the safe!" ordered Wolfie. My father, now realizing who Wolfie was, felt confused. "Wolfie, thank God it's you!" he exclaimed.

"Never mind Jew, get up and open the safe!" the German barked.

"Wolfie, we were wondering what ever happened to you? I thought maybe you were afraid we were going to circumcise you, so you ran off!" my father halfheartedly joked.

"Get up and open the safe!" Wolfie once again shouted. He pointed his pistol at my father's head and kicked him in the stomach.

"Leave my father alone!" I shouted, and I threw myself on top of my father.

Wolfie reached down, grabbed me by the back of my shirt and hoisted me up as if he were picking up a cat by the skin from the back of its neck. "Where is your piece of shit friend Benny? I've been looking for him. I have a little score to settle and I'm going to shut his big mouth up for good when I find him!" he exclaimed.

"You will never shut him up. He is too clever for you to catch him!" I replied.

He became angrier, and his blue eyes began to bulge. He started slapping and punching me, as his henchman held me, not allowing me to fall to the ground!

"Where is he?! Where is he?!!" Wolfie shouted.

"Wait a minute comrade, let's have a *schnapps* and talk about this reasonably!" interjected my father.

Wolfie suddenly stopped and cocked his pistol, motioning my father to the safe in our secret room. My father regretfully got up and paused momentarily in front of the safe, then he looked back at us as if he was contemplating something in his mind before he continued, and then he began fumbling with the combination.

"Hurry up!" Wolfie shouted.

He finally opened the heavy door and the soldiers pushed my father aside.

Wolfie stepped towards the front of the safe. He carefully inspected its contents. Then he slowly opened the tiny drawers until he found what he was looking for-- my special watch.

His face lit up as he picked it up.

"Do you think this will look good on me, Joseph?" he asked.

He gazed over at me as he fastened it on his wrist.

Another German emptied the safe's contents into a cloth sack. All our valuables were taken by those animals, as we stood paralyzed and watched. The SS soldiers then forced us up the stairs into the shop, hitting and pushing us with their guns.

My grandfather finally had enough. He charged towards Wolfie, grasping for the watch.

That ticking sound in my head began to get louder and louder, slower and slower. Time itself seemed to slow down. My grandfather was hit on the face with the butt of a rifle and knocked down.

"You Germans are the sludge of the sewers!" my grandfather growled.

Wolfie raised his pistol to my grandfather's head. My father begged Wolfie not to shoot when suddenly all the clocks began to loudly chime. Wolfie pulled the trigger, instantly killing my grandfather. My sister began to scream through the chiming. It was so loud! The whole ordeal seemed surreal.

Tick. Tick. Tick. Thundered in my head! My mother shrieked, but it was the type of cry you have in a nightmare where you scream as loud as you can, but nothing comes out. Everything was happening in slow motion as Wolfie then turned to my grandmother who was hysterically screaming with her hands-on top of her head!

"You'll burn in hell you bastards!" she shouted.

Tick. Tick. Tick. He fired two bullets into her chest!

As Wofie put another bullet into her head, she fell dead, next to my grandfather's motionless body. We were stunned and in shock as we were brutally pushed out the front door by the Gestapo henchmen.

I desperately looked over my shoulder to get the last glimpse of my grandparents lying on the floor of our shop as Wolfie's Gestapo scum ransacked our store.

***

Out on the street, my father and I were separated from my mother and little sister.

The rain had just stopped. The air was heavy with humidity.

We were forced into a covered truck and I overheard Wolfie telling a black- haired SS Captain to take my mother and sister to the woods.

The Captain began hitting my mother hard with his stick and shouted, "Run Jew swine!" She was holding Hanna, but she refused to run. Instead she walked composed and with dignity, clutching Hanna tightly to her chest. The captain continued beating her as hard as he could, she buckled over many times and almost collapsed but she did not yield to the degradation of the German and continued to calmly walk to the other truck.

"Hanna, Sarah I love you!" my father screamed over and over, until a German entered the back of the truck and hit him across the mouth with his gun. He fell to the floor still repeating "I love you, I love you my darlings!" and sobbed.

The truck began to move. I kneeled down and cradled my father's head, consoling him and begging him to pull it together. For that moment I felt that I had just become the father. Instead of my father consoling me, I was looking after him. I helped him up onto the bench seat and he regained some composure.

We sat silently as we rode through the streets of our city. In a daze, conscious but mentally unconscious, unable to comprehend what had just happened to our family.

Then the ticking stopped.

The truck screeched to a hard stop and we were thrown forward.

Polish policemen, who were now working for the Germans were waiting, they shouted at us and ordered us to get off the truck. They began pushing and hitting us mercilessly with their heavy wooden batons as we stumbled off the truck.

My father recognized one of the guards, who worked for the city picking up our trash. He called out his name. "Alexander it's me Joseph, your friend from the watch shop!" cried my father.

Stunned to hear his name, Alex paused for a moment. Realizing that he recognized my father he stopped the men. "Oh yes Joseph, what a pleasure it is to see you! For years I picked up your Jew garbage and not once did you ever give me a nice gift from your store! It's okay. Don't worry about it. We have a very nice place for you and your boy here. Comrades this Jew is special. Make sure you get him whatever he needs. Put him in the first-class accommodations and make sure he gets a thick piece of roast beef with carrots for supper," he sarcastically said.

My father caught on quickly that things were going to get ugly. Alex pushed my father down into the mud and made us crawl through the gutter to the main gate of the ghetto. He was shouting, kicking and beating us with his heavy baton as we desperately tried to get up and move into the entrance.

My father told me to hurry and pulled me through the gutter! Once we made it into the compound, they left us alone. The barbed wire gates closed behind us.

My father took hold of me and asked if I was all right.

I told him my back hurt, but I was okay.

"This is getting very bad, Koby. We have to get out of here and find your mother and sister."

A few Jewish men rushed over and helped us up. They were also prisoners of the ghetto. Desperately they asked if we had any news. Were the Russians or Americans coming to rescue them? But we knew nothing. They brought us to a rundown building and into a room where there were several other men trying to survive in this one small space.

My father told me to sit on the floor against a wall while he went to converse with some of the others.

As I sat in a state of shock, my mind drifted back to the fact that this was really happening to us. My grandparents were murdered by Wolfie and my family was torn apart.

I was afraid for us, but even more for my mother and sister.

My father returned. He gave me a piece of hard stale bread that one of the men had given him.

"Aren't you going to have some Papa?" I asked.

He said he wasn't hungry.

By now it was midnight and very dark.

My father sat down against a wall and I placed my head on his lap.

He caressed my hair and told me not to worry. He was going to fix those bastards.

"Tomorrow we will find a way to get to Mother and little Hanna." he adamantly stated.

As impossible as the situation was, I managed to drift off, despite the noise and uncomfortable hard floor beneath me.

***

I awoke the next morning to the sound of large trucks and the shouting of German soldiers in the street.

At first, I prayed that this was all a bad dream. And that when I opened my eyes I would be back at home with my family.

Unfortunately this was not a bad dream but a nightmare.

We cautiously looked out the window. Men from the ghetto were being loaded onto the trucks. The German soldiers were beating them as they tried to comply with their orders.

One old man was shot dead as he stopped to tie his shoe and another when he asked where they were going.

"Where are they taking them, father?" I asked.

He shook his head. "I don't know, but wherever they are going it couldn't be good".

Things seemed to settle down after the soldiers left and people began wandering out into the dreary streets. My father knew many of the people there, but no one knew anything about where the women and children were.

As I followed my father through the streets I suddenly recognized a man. It was Benny's father, the *shecket*! He was walking in a daze and was startled when I approached him.

"Mr. Steinfeld! It's me, Koby! Where is Benny?!" I shouted.

He looked at me and his eyes widened.

"Jacob! Are you okay? When did you get here?" he desperately questioned.

I told him how Wolfie came for us last night and murdered my grandparents and sent my mother and sister to the woods.

I was worried about Benny too, since I knew Wolfie was looking for him. "A gang of SS officers broke into our house and started beating us. Then a blue-eyed German Gestapo officer came in! He said he had a score to settle with Benny. Benny taunted him, you know how Benny is," he exclaimed.

"How could a midget shit like you become a Major? Your mother must have screwed a hundred Nazi colonels for that to happen!" Benny jeered.

"The officer became enraged and went for Benny's throat with his bare hands. But Benny had my *chalaf* hidden behind his back. He swung it hard as he came at him, striking his neck! They began shooting at Benny, but he escaped through the window and ran off!"

"I don't know where he is but I'm glad he got away. They dragged my beloved wife one way and me the other. I don't know where she is either!" cried Mr. Steinfeld.

"That blue-eyed German must have been Wolfie," I said. My father came over and told me we had to move on before the guards noticed us.

"If you find Benny tell him something for me. Tell him I love him and one more thing: 'Short and sharp.' He'll understand what that means," said Mr. Steinfeld.

I nodded and we hugged before we went our separate ways.

We wandered around the ghetto looking for any way out of the barbed wire. So many guards and the sharp barbed wire made it impossible to climb through. It was getting late and beginning to get dark.

"We had better get back to the room," said my father.

On our way back we happened to get very close to the ghetto's gate. It was open to let trucks in for the evening. There were Polish policemen standing around, smoking and drinking vodka, while dozens of empty transport trucks were pulling into the compound.

As we wandered close to the gate, my father recognized another guard who was once a customer at our shop. His name was Henry.

The guard recognized my father and beckoned us over with a motion from his rifle.

"Well fancy seeing you here Joseph!" joked the guard.

My father reached out his hand. "Better me than you, right Henry?" my father exclaimed.

And the guard laughed as they shook hands.

"How's your watch working?" questioned my father in an attempt to make conversation.

"Well to be honest it started losing time a few weeks ago. You didn't do such a good job fixing it!" he said.

"Henry, I fixed that watch five years ago!" my father kidded.

"Henry do you know of the place in the woods where they brought the women and children?" he continued.

Suddenly, the man's demeanor changed

"There was no place in the woods for living-- only for dying," he said.

"In fact, comrade, in the morning they are going to take all of you from this ghetto to the woods as well," stated Henry solemnly.

Before I had a chance to comprehend what he had said, my father struck Henry with the hardest blow I had ever seen anyone hit. As Henry fell to the ground my father grabbed my arm and shouted, "Run!" He pulled me and we ran through the open gate as more trucks poured into the compound.

Guards began shooting at us. We could hear the bullets flying by our heads! Sirens went off and they released their dogs who were fiercely barking and chasing after us. When you are running for your life, it's amazing how fast you can run!

My father kept hold of me and shouted, "We're heading for the river!"

Two of the savage German shepherd guard dogs were rapidly gaining on us, and I could hear their vicious barking and teeth snapping right at our heels!

The ferocious animals finally caught up with us just as we leapt off the embankment into the raging river. However, their pursuit didn't just end at the river's edge, and they continued on their ferocious attack as they dove after us, snapping their razor-sharp teeth and then latching on to us in midair! When we hit the water, my father quickly subdued the dog that was attacking him by holding its head under water and he drowned him! Recent rains had engorged the river and the filthy water was flowing faster than I had ever seen. The dog that was relentlessly holding onto my shirt sleeve began to struggle in the water and was beginning to have difficulty staying afloat. Quickly, I grabbed his collar and held his head above the water. As much as that dog wanted to kill me, I didn't have the heart to let him drown.

My father held on to me and I held onto the dog never letting go, as we were swept away by the raging current down river. We were tossed about for some time and as soon as we were out of sight we made our way to the river's bank. I dragged the unconscious dog onto the shore, and my father picked up a large rock.

"What are you going to do with that rock?" I exclaimed.

"I'm going to smash that dog's skull in before he wakes up and realizes he didn't finish his job," my father stated.

I turned away not to watch but then I noticed my father's arms become heavy, and as hard as he tried...he couldn't do it.

I saw that the dog had a collar with a metal tag on it.

"What's his name, Papa?" I asked.

My father read the tag and replied, "Katzchen."

He looked at me dumbfoundedly.

"This dog's name is Kitten," he remarked. If we weren't in so much trouble I might have laughed at that. But instead I just shook my head in disbelief.

He laid there unconscious and my father found a piece of twine and wrapped it around his muzzle and tied him up to a large sapling that was growing out of the ground.

"Just in case he wakes up with bad intentions," my father stated.

We realized that if we were caught again, we would surely be killed.

"Papa, do you think it was true what Henry said about the woods?" I asked.

"I don't believe that they would kill women and little children, no one is that evil," my father replied.

"While it's still dark, let's go see if we can find them," father said.

We crawled up the bank and began walking through the muddy bog which abutted the river. Hidden by the darkness we made our way to the only wooded area we knew outside of town, "The Willows."

It was a place where we would sometimes go hiking and see some of the wildlife in the woods. Some people would even vacation there. As we approached, we heard the rumble of bulldozers and saw bright lights.

The area was hilly. We carefully crawled up an embankment, which overlooked the site. Bulldozers were digging large deep trenches. We could see a mountain of small brown rocks and another one with colored paper.

"What do you make of those big piles of rocks and paper?" I asked my father.

"It's not rocks and paper, Koby. Those are shoes and clothes," he mournfully stated.

Just then a row of transport trucks pulled onto the site. SS guards shouted and whipped the men, women and children as they were ordered off the trucks. They were forced to quickly undress, and their shoes and clothing were added to the large piles.

Then they were rushed up the hill to line up naked along the top of the open trench, where they faced Nazi Gestapo assassins dressed in black and wielding machine guns.

Most were in a state of shock. Most didn't even resist, hoping that obeying would save their lives. The few that did attempt to fight were gunned down where they stood.

Men, women and children held each other and screamed as the Nazi death squad began mercilessly gunning them down with their machine guns and they fell recklessly into the trench alongside the other dead victims!

That sound I will never forget.

My father put his head down and we both cried.

We now knew they were evil. And we had come to realize that my mother and my poor little sister must have been killed in the same manner, by these heartless blood thirsty bastards.

We made our way back to the river and returned to the remote area of the swamp where we had left the dog. The twine was chewed through and the dog was gone.

Maybe it was a blessing, we really didn't know what to expect from him upon our return.

We stayed hidden in the reeds that night and all through the next day. When night came, my father said, "We have to make our way back to the shop."

"The shop! Are you crazy! If we go back there they will find us and kill us for sure!" I shouted.

"Never mind, Koby. There is something important we need to get, otherwise we will be dead anyway," he said.

When it got even darker, we cautiously made our way out of the swamp and headed towards town.

The streets were mostly deserted. Whenever we saw anyone, we would hide among the trash left in the streets or disappear into one of the numerous vacant buildings along the way.

I kept wondering what was so important that we had to risk our lives to get back to the shop, but I knew better than to question my father.

When we finally arrived at the shop, we found the door had been left open. It was eerie going in. The broken glass shards sparkled on the floor and crunched under my feet.

I wandered to the front of the store, where the only thing left was the broken display cases and the bloodstained floor where my grandparents had been murdered.

I stared at the spot, reliving the atrocity. I laid down on the floor, as if absorbing their blood would bring them back to me.

My father came looking for me and he asked me to rise. As I stood up, I noticed the doorbell was on the floor, and I picked it up. For no logical reason, I hung it back on the door, where it had always been. It was the only remnant from the past that remained.

We carefully walked down the stairs into the basement. It was dark. Whatever my father had said he needed was apparently there. Suddenly we heard the front door open! The bell, which I had just placed on it, jingled. We could hear footsteps above. Things were being pushed around.

We froze as a beam of light from a flashlight broke through the darkness and lit up the staircase.

A man carrying a rifle appeared! We tried dropping down on the floor and hiding. But we were caught! There was no chance to run.

The man began to speak, in an angry voice.

"Everyone has been looking for you two Jews!" he said.

We looked up, partially blinded by the flashlight, realizing it was not a soldier. Rather, it was Alexander, the terrible Polish guard from the ghetto!

"I had a feeling you two would return back to your Jew nest! And now I'll collect the hefty bounty the Germans placed on your two asses!" he laughed. Our hearts became heavy as we realized that there was no way out. We were doomed.

"The Germans are going to cut off your balls and hang you upside down with piano wire for their dogs to rip you apart," taunted Alex. "Maybe I'll take your jewels home and grind them up and make sausages out of them. They're kosher, right?" he chuckled.

Just then he noticed the entrance to our secret hiding room. "Where does that door lead to?" he questioned.

"It's just a door that goes nowhere," replied my father.

Suspecting there might be some sort of treasure behind the door, he motioned us away from it with his gun.

"You must have come back here for something," he said.

With his back he forcefully pushed on the door while holding the flashlight in one hand, the gun on us with the other. Slowly the door creaked open a bit. Facing us, he continued to back into the room, carefully keeping his gun trained on us.

As he backed up and crossed the threshold, the door got stuck. Alex pushed on it harder, banging against it over and over with his back, struggling to push it open. He became frustrated as he repeatedly tried to unjam it.

Suddenly, a large arm reached from behind the door. It grabbed Alexander by the hair, pulling his head back, then delivered a decisive slash across his throat with a long flat blade! The flashlight fell from Alex's hand, spinning on the floor and casting light in all directions.

Alex's eyes bulged out of his head in agony as his blood gushed from his gaping wound!

I quickly ran for the flashlight and pointed it at the men. It was Benny!!

Alexander was still thrashing about, but Benny held him tightly until his blood drained out. He let go only when my father told him Alex was dead.

"Short and sharp," Benny whispered. Then he let the limp form fall to the floor and wiped the bloody blade on the body. "He got what he deserved," Benny stated.

My father and I raced towards Benny and we all hugged!

"Benny you saved us!" my father rejoiced. "How did you get here?!"

"Wolfie is a German SS Major now. He came to my house looking for me," Benny replied.

"I got him really angry. You would have been proud of me! I managed to escape. This was the only place I knew of, but you were gone."

Then he asked if we had seen his parents.

"I'm sorry to tell you but I think your mother was killed along with my mother and little sister in the woods. Wolfie came here looking for us and that's when we got caught! He killed my grandparents and he took all the watches from the safe, including the one my grandfather made for me. He then sent my father and me to the ghetto. That's where I found your father. He asked me to tell you if I found you, that he loves you very much and to remember "Short and sharp".

My father knew the guard at the gate. He told us they were going to kill everyone in the ghetto and my father hit him, that's when we escaped. I'm sorry Benny, but your father may be dead too," I sadly stated.

Benny's eyes began to tear up and he began to cry. My father put his hand on his shoulder.

"Don't worry Benny, you are not alone. From now on you are my son too. We'll take care of each other."

Benny stood up and placed his blade into a sheath that he had made out of leather.

"That son of a bitch Wolfie came to my house looking for me! But I gave him something to remember me by! I tried to chop the bastards head off, but his collar got in the way!" declared Benny.

"What did your father mean by 'Short and sharp?'" I asked.

"When we slaughter animals we have to do it quickly and humanely," but now his message means to be cunning, quick and deadly.

My father picked up Alex's rifle and began smashing the wall in the basement. Pieces of plaster were falling everywhere as he swung the rifle.

"Father, you'll ruin the only gun we have!" I shouted as the gun finally broke into pieces. "Now we don't even have a weapon!"

But that turned out not to be the case. Reaching into a large hole in the wall, to my amazement, he retrieved a dull black machine gun.

"This is why we came back!" he explained.

It didn't stop there. He continued pulling out more guns and ammunition from behind the wall! Struggling, he heaved out a large canister with back straps and a short hose connected to a gun- like handle.

"What is that, Papa?" I questioned.

"It's a flamethrower," he replied.

I had no idea my father had amassed such an arsenal of weapons.

"Papa, where did this all come from?" I asked.

"Over the years I did a lot of trades with military people for watches and watch repairs.

There is one more thing we need," he continued. He went back to the hole and pulled up a heavy cloth sack about the size of a soccer ball.

"What's in the sack?" I asked.

"Gold coins. Now let's see what we can find for supplies in the hideout room."

The room was a mess. Clothes and trash were all over the floor.

"Find something to change into, Koby. Get out of those dirty clothes," he said.

As we began fumbling through the clothing, I couldn't help getting upset again when I came across my mother's sweater and my sister's nightgown.

I clutched them to my face, desperately inhaling their scent so that I would never forget it.

We managed to find some clothes and we changed as Benny looked out. As we left, I noticed my sister's tiny slippers lying by the door. I felt so sad for her. These words came to me. With a pencil I found, I wrote them down on the wall ...

Her little shoes beside the door.
To run and skip and dance no more.

Those little shoes that cradled our love,
The little child who wore them now watches from above.

Those little shoes empty and still,
Her little heart is gone and now she never will.

The day that comes and the lord I may meet,
I'll ask him why he took from us, those tiny little feet.

My father slung three machine guns over his shoulder.

We stood there watching him as he gathered a rucksack and filled it with long clips of ammunition.

"What are you boys waiting for? Pick up as many machine guns as you can carry and fill up the rucksacks with ammunition," he ordered.

Up until this point, we had just been boys, unsure if we were even allowed to touch guns. But things were different now.

"Let me show you how these work," he said.

"Pick up a clip of bullets. Snap it into the gun frame. Pull the bolt back and let it go. It will be chambering a bullet. Then all you have to do is aim and pull the trigger until there are no more bullets. Then start all over again by pushing the release button to drop the empty clip. There is a safety button. Make sure it's in the red when you are ready to shoot," he instructed.

We eagerly filled the bags with ammunition and carried them on our backs.

Benny and I each grabbed two machine guns and we slung them over our shoulders.

There were hand grenades too. They were very heavy, so we attached those to our belts.

It's amazing how empowered a gun makes you feel. Now at least we had a chance.

The three of us quietly exited the shop for the last time. But before we departed, I took the bell from the door and stuffed it into my sack.

"Why do you want the bell?" my father asked.

"It's all we have left from the store, Papa," I replied.

We scurried out the back door and hid behind some bushes.

"Boys, we need to get away from here, but first we have something dangerous we must do," stated my father.

"Benny are you kids up to killing some Nazi bastards?" father questioned.

Benny cocked his machine gun and said, "Some? Let's kill them all!"

My father looked at me and I nodded my head in agreement.

"Okay, we are going back to the Willows," he ordered.

Lugging our arsenal we made our way, crisscrossing the streets of our lost town, being careful not to be seen by anyone.

Suddenly we stopped when we noticed a black military car with Nazi regalia parked on a side street.

The car door opened, as two transport trucks arrived loaded with SS guards.

We backed off into an alley as the trucks idled.

We saw a German SS officer meeting with a Polish townsman. He was giving the Germans directions to a Jewish hide out and collecting his reward.

My father, armed with his flamethrower, struggled with his lighter to ignite it. "I can't light this thing!" he frantically whispered in vain.

He kept fumbling with it until Benny calmly placed his hand over his and with a strike of his thumb, a large flame flared up from the lighter and the flamethrower came to life!

My father peered around the corner and nervously aimed the flame thrower at the crowd.

With a simple pull of his finger, a gigantic streak of red-hot fire blazed across the street, and exploded on them, setting them all on fire! The hot smell of gasoline and burnt flesh filled the air as the soldiers hopelessly tried to escape the flames.

The men struggled to run away! Totally on fire as they shrieked horrifically, unable to quench the flames that were consuming their bodies!

The Polish informant too met his fate, when suddenly one of the truck's gas tanks exploded and a large piece of shrapnel blew his head off! The street then became silent, except for the sound of the fire crackling and burning all that was left.

Chapter Three

We left the alley and stealthily made our way back to the Willows.

We crawled up the embankment that overlooked the killing area, resting for a moment.

Their murdering was over for the day. The executioners were making their way into a nearby barracks. It was a small two-story building which was once an old hotel. They were mocking all the people they killed: laughing, pointing their weapons, and reenacting their atrocities.

My father told us to wait as he crawled down the hill toting his flame thrower in the pitch-black night. Dozens of SS officers and guards were moving around inside the building. We could see them through the windows, eating, drinking and laughing. Relaxing after a typical day at work, with no reservations or guilt about the hundreds of innocent men, women, and children they had murdered.

As hard as we watched, we could no longer see my father, until I saw a tiny light and a small flame coming from the end of his weapon.

We peered intently over the embankment as we laid on the ground with our guns pointed below in the event he was discovered, as he approached the Nazi barracks.

Suddenly behind us we heard the breach of a rifle cock, and a tall German soldier with rotted teeth was standing there, aiming his rifle at us! He was shouting angrily in his German tongue for us to get up, but we didn't understand him! He was motioning at us with his rifle to stand, but we hesitated, and he became more aggressive, and then he aimed his gun at my head and began squeezing the trigger on his rifle!

I heard a dog barking and caught notice of a vicious guard dog racing up the hill towards us.

The animal was blood thirsty and running as fast as he could to attack us and rip us to pieces!

The Soldier began to smile and laughed heinously, when he noticed the dog rapidly racing up the hill in our direction. He became excited with anticipation. Savoring the fact that he would be witnessing our brutal and bloody death by the vicious beast!

The ferocious dog was quickly upon us, and he launched himself into the air at us. I closed my eyes anticipating his shark-like teeth ripping through my skin, but instead of attacking us, he flew completely over us and attacked the German soldier!

The German pulled the trigger on his rifle as he fell backwards and the dog latched onto him! It was a mad fight between the two of them! Until ultimately the dog finally got a hold of the Soldier's throat and ripped it apart!

The soldier laid there dying as the blood faced dog turned his attention towards us. We thought we were next, and we had our guns ready, but his tail began to wag, and his demeanor instantly changed.

I then noticed the short piece of twine dangling from his neck. It was Kitten! He staggered over to me, and I then noticed a bloody bullet hole in his chest.

He carefully laid down next to me and gently put his head down on my leg, and he slowly closed his eyes.

"How could such a vicious animal have any bit of tenderness?" I thought.

We quickly turned our attention back to my father, he was in close proximity to the barracks and was preparing to shoot, when a German SS Commander stepped outside the doorway of the building. He was holding an unlit cigar in his hand and appeared to be unsuccessfully trying to light a match.

We were petrified. Our hearts pounded but neither of us could pull the trigger on our weapons!

"Hold tight," whispered Benny.

The Commander noticed the small flame coming from the darkness and shouted to my father: "*Hast du ein Licht, freund*?" He believed my father was simply another officer, one with a match.

Since my father spoke German, he understood that the officer was asking him for a light for his cigar.

"*Ja Vol*, Herr Commander, enjoy your cigar!" replied my father.

He squeezed the trigger of the flame thrower and a gigantic fireball blasted out from its barrel! It entirely engulfed the tyrant's head! His agonizing scream was silenced by the roar of the flame as the fire melted away the skin and muscle from his face leaving only his charred skull. His flaming body quickly collapsed as he was converted into burnt ashes on the spot!

Darkness became light as my father torched the entire barracks with gigantic streams of liquefied fire!

There was hardly any noise coming from the flamethrower as my father unleashed its blazing fury, just a loud "hiss" as a snake would make before it strikes.

Everyone and everything in the barracks was on fire! The bastards horrifically screamed and flailed about, burning to death with no possible escape!

Soldiers came running from all directions with their guns drawn! Neither Benny nor I had ever held a gun before-- let alone shoot one-- but we pulled our triggers. The guns became alive, cranking out storms of bullets.

Meanwhile my father continued to unleash the flamethrower on everything in his path including the bulldozers and trucks until his weapon died out and was totally out of fuel.

The burning was so bright we could see my father quickly discarding the tank on his back and making his way up the embankment to us. We kept on showering the area with bullets, mowing down every Nazi we could see!

"Short and sharp!" exclaimed Benny.

Clumsily we stood up with our arsenal of weapons clanking against us, and I noticed "Kitten" was lying there motionless. He had died saving me from the very people that trained him to hunt and kill us. There was no time to mourn him, but I kissed him on top of his head and removed the piece of twine from his neck. I'll never forget "Kitten" and the sacrifice he made for us, and we quickly left to meet up with my father.

***

We felt some satisfaction that we had been able to kill some of those devils, but it was not enough for what they had done to our people and our families.

In the distance we could hear their dogs barking. The sky was lit up from the massive fire.

The Nazi's will be looking for us.

"We have to get back into the river. We need to lose the dogs!" said my father.

He sent Benny and me to search for something that could keep us afloat. In the nearby marsh filled with swamp grass, we discovered a small rowboat that was damaged and inoperable. It was filled with small holes and we were worried it would never float. However, we decided we should bring it back since it was all we could find.

My father was waiting for us impatiently. He had found a large truck tire floating in the swamp.

"Papa, this was all we could find. It was hard searching in the dark. The boat is filled with holes," I said.

"Never mind, Koby. I have an idea. We are heading back to the river. Put all the supplies into the boat," he said.

We began our journey through the swamp, we pushed the boat over the thick heavy mud and swamp grass back to the river. As we neared the river, we could hear the water still raging as it meandered through its course.

We approached a plot near the river that was laden with rubbish. We found a long-broken crate, which my father instructed me to put in the boat, as well. I was unsure of what his idea was, but it was all in God's will, I thought.

By now it must have been past midnight and the cloudy sky blocked the moon's light as we got to the river's edge.

"Koby, give me the tire and the crate," ordered my father.

He floated the tire on top of the water and placed the crate on top of it. That measure kept the crate off the water's surface.

"Now put all the guns and ammunition in the crate," he instructed.

We did what we were told. My father then told us to turn the boat upside down. He helped us place it on top of the crate concealing it. It fit perfectly, and it looked like a junk capsized boat floating on the water.

"Let's go, boys. We'll hide under the boat as we float down the river."

We heard their mad dogs barking in the distance as we entered the water. We hid under the capsized boat and took hold and kept our heads up. We began floating down the rough current, which quickly carried us down the river.

Hidden by darkness, we used our bodies as rudders to guide the boat. The water was cold, but we had to tolerate it.

After a few hours, just before dawn, we found a hiding spot in the reeds along the bank. It appeared that we were several miles outside of town, in a boggy area.

We were cold, wet, hungry and lucky to be alive.

The only food available to us was frogs, snails and leeches.

Benny and I caught as many frogs as we could. We pulled off the leeches, which attached themselves to our skin, and put them all in a large tin can my father had found.

He used a stick and mashed them into a gooey gruel.

"It's ready," he said.

As hungry as we were, none of us were prepared to take the first bite.

My father, growing impatient, ordered Benny and me to eat.

"Papa, you should go first, since you made this delicious meal! After all Papa, one of the Ten Commandments states, 'Children must honor their parents' and it would be an honor if you go first!" I chuckled.

"Very funny, Koby, but what that commandment really means is, 'You had better listen to what your father tells you.' Now eat!"

It was strange that despite everything we had been through, that we still could laugh.

I looked over at Benny, who was content watching my father and me fight it out.

"You heard *our* Papa. Now eat!" I ordered.

Benny gave in and picked up the can. He stared at the contents before mustering up his nerve.

"There are eyeballs staring back at me!" he squawked. He closed his eyes and scooped out a glob of gruel with his two fingers, placing it in his mouth. He closed lips over his gooey fingers and pulled them out of his mouth leaving the gruel behind.

My father and I watched intently. We felt his pain as we waited for his reaction. He struggled to chew, then swallowed hard and wiped his mouth with his sleeve. "Well?" I impatiently asked.

A strange look came over him as he clutched his stomach. Then he fell over backwards and passed out!

"Papa, Benny's dead! You killed him!" I shouted.

After a bit, Benny recovered and slowly opened his eyes. He coughed and spoke gravely...

"It tastes like chicken."

"I knew you were faking it!" I chuckled.

We all agreed that at worst it tasted swampy and needed salt.

We hid in the swamp grass for the remainder of the day, listening carefully for anyone who might stumble upon us. We kept quiet and out of sight.

When darkness came again, we resumed our journey down the river heading toward the open countryside.

As we drifted, from underneath the boat we would occasionally see soldiers on the riverbank staring at our capsized boat, but no one paid much attention to it. We continued on down the river for some time but unfortunately our luck seemed to run out, as we approached a large train trestle, which spanned the river.

Dozens of German soldiers perched with their guns were scanning the river from the bridge with a large spotlight. The dogs must have led them to the riverbank, where they lost our scent. They knew we were somewhere in the water. The current was too swift, and we couldn't stop or drift towards shore!

My father ordered us to take machine guns and choose a hole in the hull of the boat to shoot from.

"Benny, to the left bank. Koby to the right bank. And I'll take the bridge," he ordered.

I became numb. My stomach hurt. The "ticking" in my head began once again. That rhythm brings me to another place. A place where it extinguishes my emotions and fear when I am in danger.

Tick. Tick. Tick. Tick.

When the danger intensifies, the ticking slows. And the slower it ticks, the stronger I get. My senses become sharper. Everything seems to happen in slow motion. When I hear the ticking, it is as if I become someone else.

As we drifted toward the bridge, the spotlight honed in on our capsized boat.

We heard a German shout something and the soldiers swarmed the riverbank aiming their guns at us.

A Commander drew his pistol and began shooting at us! We could hear the bullets whizzing by us, but fortunately none hit us. Some did impact the water near us, but to my surprise, they just stopped at the surface and never made it through the water.

A few soldiers laughed and lowered their arms, taking notice how badly the Commander was shooting.

I noticed a teenage boy holding a hunting rifle on the riverbank. He watched intently as we drifted by. He appeared bloodthirsty, watching for the Germans, hoping to help them kill some Jews.

Almost feeling that we were going to make it past the gauntlet of soldiers, I suddenly noticed Benny's yarmulke floating next to him in the water.

"Benny, your yarmulke!" I whispered in panic.

He grabbed for it in the dark, but it managed to slip through his fingers and disappeared under the dark water and then arose outside our boat.

The searchlights were still scanning over us when suddenly the reflection of the silver Star of David embroidered on Benny's yarmulke lit up and caught the eye of the Polish teenager.

"*Juden*!!" he shouted, and he was wildly pointing at us.

"NOW!" my father ordered. We all pulled our triggers and our machine guns spat out their bullets on the unsuspecting soldiers. The noise was deafening as our guns cranked out bullets. I was getting hit with Benny's red-hot empty shells, as they ejected from his gun. My father shot at the spotlight and began mowing down everyone on the bridge. The three of us were firing away as the German soldiers were falling into the water, dead.

I watched the Polish boy who had pointed us out. He was shooting at us and jumping up and down erratically.

"Kill them! Kill them! They are getting away!" he shouted.

Without any hesitation, I put a bullet into his chest. That was the last shot I fired. I watched him flail and fall backwards to the ground. I felt no remorse killing that piece-of-shit boy. None.

The current suddenly became violent, as we passed under the bridge. We were propelled through the rapids. The soldiers continued firing at us, but we quickly disappeared into the darkness. The swift current carried us for some time down river until my father felt it was time for us to leave the water.

"We have to let this boat go and get out of the river!" he said.

While still under the boat, we struggled to get ourselves to the river's edge. Once we were able to feel the river's bottom with our feet, we pushed ourselves ashore.

We lifted the boat off the crate and removed all our weapons and gear.

We put the overturned boat back on the crate and pushed it back into the water. It quickly disappeared down the river. I felt as if we were as lost as that boat. Would it wander aimlessly? Would it make it to the sea? Or would it just sink?

My father decided we should make our way south, where there wouldn't be as many German sympathizers.

The fact was, besides Wolfie, no one knew if we were Jews or not.

It would only take our Polish friends and neighbors to turn on us.

What someone could do for a bag of sugar or a pound of bacon was deplorable. I'll never forget what those bastards did to us. Never!

***

We were wet and filthy, but we found a secluded spring in the woods, where we could rest.

Somehow my father's lighter worked, and we were able to make a small campfire to dry our clothes. We sat on large rocks by the fire naked while our clothes dried. No one spoke a word. We just sat there and stared into the fire. There was nothing to say. We just sat there motionless. In the distance we could hear the repeated blasts of a train's steam whistle, and I wished I was on that train to somewhere else.

"Where are we going to go?" asked Benny, breaking the silence.

"We have to hide by day and travel by night. And find safe places where no one will find us. Somehow, we must get to America, maybe south through Italy. I'm not sure," said my father.

"America?" I scoffed. "How are we going to get halfway around the world if we can't even get away from what's around us here?"

"God will help us," replied my father.

I shook my head in disbelief while Benny watched.

My father and Benny began collecting our clothes, but I refused to get up.

"What do we have to live for, Papa? They killed Mama and Hanna and *Bubby* and *Zaydee* and Benny's parents too! They will catch us and kill us too, and hang us, like Alexander said!" I cried.

Benny came over and helped me up, while my father gathered our things.

"Come on, Koby, we made it this far. At least maybe we can take down some more of those Nazi bastards before they get us. Short and sharp."

I shook my head and stood up reluctantly. Then once again we began traveling through the night.

***

We were hungry as we made our way south through the woods, crawling through briars and tripping on rocks. It was difficult to travel in the dark, and not being familiar with our surroundings. We had no compass or means to navigate.

The only basis that we knew to get a bearing of our direction was the green moss growing on the north side of tree stumps. Other than the moss, we had nothing else to rely on.

We knew we were being hunted by the Nazi's after all the death and destruction we had caused them.

It was an embarrassment to them and their regime. That one Jew watchmaker and his two children were able to create so much havoc, and kill so many Nazi's all on their own.

They had to be desperately trying to find us, and surely they would make an example out of us as Alex had boasted.

We occasionally heard their vicious dogs barking and gunshots in the distance.

They were tracking us, and it kept us moving. It was now a different time than we were accustomed to. Any mistake could cost us our lives.

In the distance, I could still hear the incessant blasts of the steam trains whistle, and it began to haunt us as it persisted every hour on the hour, like precision German clockwork. People moving freely, maybe going on a holiday, but not us. We weren't that lucky.

As we plodded through the forest I had plenty of time to think about the loss of my mother, little sister and my grandparents.

Although, I'm lucky to be here with my father, I wished he was more like my mother. Soft, attentive, and loving. I miss her so much.

By dawn the following morning we had stumbled on an area in the woods where the soil had given way, and several massive oak trees had fallen over and were rotting along the forest floor.

We were able to peel off large wide strips of dead tree bark and we used them as sort of a "Bark blanket" to cover and conceal us as we laid down along the length of the fallen tree trunks and tried to get some rest that day.

Lying motionless and trying to sleep during the day was difficult.

We were being plagued by ants, termites and bees. Along with an occasional snake throughout the day, as we hid under the bark and dead trees.

At one point, late in the afternoon, we heard a man conversing with a woman in polish approximately 20 meters from where we were hiding.

They were frolicking through the woods enjoying the day, when they noticed the area of fallen trees and decided to investigate them.

My father and I were close to each other, but Benny was lying along a separate tree about 2 meters away.

Their voices became louder as the couple approached us, and from a little hole in the bark I could see them coming.

They seemed to be in their mid-twenties. The woman was very pretty and had blond hair. The man was handsome and was wearing a hat pinned with a small bird's feather that he must have found along the way. They were romantically holding hands as they walked towards us, being careful not to trip.

"Keep still, they don't have guns, but if they discover us we will have to kill them! They could report us for a reward to the Nazi's," my father whispered.

I held my breath as they were just about on top of us.

The man was flirtatious, suggesting to his girlfriend that there was no one around, and he always wanted to get naked in the forest with a beautiful woman.

She laughed and told him he was crazy! And he led her over to the other tree that Benny was hiding against.

They sat down on the tree trunk unaware that we were hiding near them, and especially that Benny was right underneath them, concealed under his bark cover!

The conversation quickly ended, and it became very quiet.

I heard subtle sounds of clothing being tossed onto a bush. But then it got louder, and we heard all sorts of kissing and slobbering, grunting and groaning taking place on the tree!

It was extremely difficult for me to control my laughter for I knew Benny must be doing everything in his power to contain himself as well!

After a while the couple stopped, and they began speaking again.

Suddenly the faint sound of the distant trains steam whistle blasted once again, and the woman asked the man if he knew where that train was going?

The man paused.

"The Germans are filling cattle cars to the brim with thousands of Jews. Their whole families, even children," the man sadly stated.

"Oh no, where are they taking them? Are they being deported to another country?!" she questioned.

"Unfortunately not. They are taking them to Treblinka to be murdered in a killing factory," the man mournfully stated.

The woman became visibly upset and they quickly left.

I guess maybe I was too young to process that information, and I couldn't stop thinking about their romantic encounter.

We stayed hidden there for the rest of the afternoon, and I couldn't wait to hear what Benny's rendition of the whole ordeal was going to be like!

Oddly, my father and I had been together the entire day and he had hardly spoken a word to me.

I'm beginning to wonder if he would have preferred that I was the one taken away to the woods, and Moma and Hana were here with him now. That's how he is behaving towards me, cold and distant.

Several times throughout the day I heard him weeping, as we hid under the bark. I guess he didn't feel like talking or he had nothing to say.

He was sad and thinking about losing our family to the German henchmen.

But there was something I just couldn't get out of my mind, and I was becoming more and more disgruntled with him.

My father had an arsenal of weapons hidden in the basement wall of the watch shop.

Why didn't he have a gun in our hiding place?

That could have changed everything, and everyone might still be alive if he hadn't been so negligent!

We tried to sleep for the rest of the afternoon, and when dusk finally fell, my father and I crawled out of our hiding place. We were covered with bug bites, bits of leaves and decomposed wood.

Benny heard us rummaging about, and comically he peeked over the tree trunk at me and we both burst out laughing!

My father was a little embarrassed about the man and woman situation, but he was acting distressed and visibly upset about something.

"Stop laughing! Didn't you hear what that man said about the trains! They are murdering our people! Our friends and families by the thousands! Shipped in cattle cars like animals to the slaughter!" my father shouted.

We instantly stopped carrying on, and just then we heard another set of long blasts from the steam trains ominous whistle.

***

It was our second night on the run, and we were very hungry. Occasionally we found some wild berries or mushrooms, but it was dark, and we were unsure if they were poisonous or edible.

The steam trains distant whistle was a constant reminder that the Nazi's were the epitome of evil and it was frustrating that we couldn't stop them.

After traveling for a few hours, we came across a quiet shallow stream meandering through the forest, and we stopped for a drink.

We were barely there for 2 minutes when my father ordered Benny and me to get up and keep moving.

Benny quickly jumped up, but I continued to just sit there.

"Jacob, come on, let's go!" My father firmly ordered.

"No, I'm not ready yet," I smugly replied.

My father immediately recognized that I was disrespecting him and he walked over and grabbed me by the back of my shirt and hoisted me up.

When he let go of my shirt, I dropped back onto the ground!

"What's gotten into you?!" he exclaimed.

"I don't think you know where the hell you are going! For all we know you are just taking us around in circles!" I exclaimed.

"Oh sure, here we go again. Jacob the complainer!" my father shouted.

"That's right I am the complainer! Somebody has to have the courage to speak up around here!" I shouted and glanced at Benny.

"I got us this far smartass! And if it wasn't for me, we all would be dead right now!" my father shouted.

"It's because of you that Mother, Hanna, Bubbie and Zaydee ARE DEAD!!" I screamed.

My father was stunned at my statement!

"Come on Jacob, it wasn't Papa's fault," Benny softly interjected.

"Shut up Benny, he's not your father!" I shouted with unyielding anger.

Benny just sadly dropped his head as if I had punched him in the stomach and wandered away from us.

My father became quiet and stared deeply into my eyes.

"How was it *my* fault that they were killed?" he somberly asked.

"You had an arsenal of weapons hidden in a wall outside our secret hiding place!

Did it ever occur to you that the guns should have been "in" the room with us so we could get to them!

When Wolfie came with his army of Gestapo and found us, we could have killed those bastards before they did what they did to our family!" I exclaimed.

My father nodded his head in disbelief. Now he understood why I was so frustrated, and he tried to put his arms around me, but I stepped back, and he became stern once again.

"Let me tell you something, Koby!"

"First of all, no one could imagine in a million years that the Germans could be so diabolical and evil, to take up murdering innocent men, women and children.

The worst that we could imagine was that we would be deported out of the country.

The second thing was, your mother was deathly afraid of guns. She knew I had the arsenal, but she insisted that it was too dangerous to have guns around children.

She was adamant about it, and would not let me bring a gun into the secret room.

Thirdly, I didn't listen to her, and behind the safe I had a machine gun concealed with my prayer shawl over it. If you remember I paused before I opened the safe. I contemplated grabbing the machine gun and shooting them all!

But there were to many Nazi's that raided our store that night!

I knew that if I pulled the gun out, they would have killed everyone instantly.

This way I thought we at least had a chance to live," my father solemnly stated.

I listened to his words intently, and then I began to feel terrible about what I had said to him and Benny.

My emotions suddenly began to overwhelm me.

Just when I thought that I had no more tears left in my body, I began to cry uncontrollably.

My father took me in his arms and held me close, and tried to comfort me in the way my mother used to do.

"I love you Koby with all my might, never forget that. I'm just so worried about your Mother and Hana," my father cried.

"I'm sorry Papa, I'm so stupid sometimes," and I continued crying.

"Yes, you are stupid, more than just sometimes though!" snickered Benny.

"I'm sorry Benny, I really didn't mean what I said. We are a family now, and I'm proud to call you my brother," I sniffled.

We all hugged, and I saw things in a different light. My father is my hero, and so we continued off on our journey once again.

Chapter Four

It was approximately midnight when we came across a meadow and saw a small farm. There wasn't much to it but a small barn and a little dilapidated house.

We could hear a cow mooing and some pigs rummaging around.

"Maybe we can take a pig to eat." suggested my father.

"A pig! Can't we take the cow! I don't know how to kill a pig! And to be honest, I think I would rather go back to eating frogs and snails than eat pig meat!" declared Benny.

We hid the guns and ammunition in an old hollowed-out tree near the edge of the meadow and snuck down to the farm.

It felt good not to have to lug the heavy rifles, and ammunition. But we were still carrying our pistols, just in case we needed them. It was about midnight and it was eerie walking about the farm.

My father pushed open the barn door. The heavy smell of animal urine and dung filled our noses. He took inventory of the animals.

"There is one cow, four pigs and several hens. As hungry as we are, I feel bad taking an animal from this poor farmer," he whispered.

"Let's just take some eggs, then. The farmer will never miss them," said Benny.

We stumbled around in the dark, feeling the nests for eggs, not realizing that hens only lay during the morning's light. However, there were no eggs to be found. The hens became agitated and caused a stir as we searched their nests. "Forget it! Let's just take a hen!" exclaimed Benny.

Just then, the barn door suddenly swung open. A man with a lantern stood there. It was the farmer, responding to the ruckus. He froze as he realized he was outnumbered and had no weapon.

"Please don't shoot me. I'm only a poor farmer and a father!" he begged.

My father told the man to settle down.

"We're not going to harm you, sir. We are looking for some food and then we will be on our way. Can you spare a few eggs?" he asked.

"You ask me with guns pointed at my head for something you can just take. Believe me, comrade, I have three girls and a sickly wife who need me. If all you want is a few eggs to settle your hunger, I will get them for you, but please do not harm us."

My father gazed at the man, who seemed familiar to him. "What is your name, farmer?" questioned my father.

"I am Dombrovsky," he replied.

My father's eyes widened! "Now I recognize you! You came to my watch shop a few years back, selling butter for money to buy shoes for your children!"

Dombrovsky gazed back at my father, and quickly realizing this filthy bearded man was the watchmaker who showed him some kindness when no one else would.

"Yes! I remember you!!" he exclaimed.

The two men hugged each other as if they were long lost friends.

"What's going on? Why aren't you back in Vilna at your watch shop?" Dombrovsky queried.

"Friend, the Germans are killing the Jews all over the country. They came into Vilna and began rounding up and murdering all the Jewish men, women and children.

"They killed my wife and little girl and now they are looking for us. We have been on the run for days and have not eaten, except for some frogs and leeches from the river," continued my father.

Dombrovsky's eyes became somber. His voice softened.

"I'm so sorry, Watchmaker. We are isolated from the city, but I have heard of these atrocities. The Germans have been here looking for Jews, but they left quickly. Who are these two boys with you?" he asked.

"They are my sons," my father replied, glancing at Benny and smiling.

"Stay here tonight in my barn. I will get you some food and drink," Dombrovsky said and he left for the farm house.

"Boys go back to the woods and get the guns. I don't know if we can trust this man. He is very poor and may send word out that he has found us, for a reward. We cannot trust anyone," warned my father.

We ran out of the barn and made our way back to the woods and retrieved our guns. Upon our return we hid them in a haystack in the barn. Dombrovsky had just returned with a loaf of bread and butter, a bowl full of soft-boiled eggs and a half-eaten chicken.

"Here let me get you some milk," he said. He placed a small wooden pail under his cow and sat on a short three-legged stool and grasped its udders. He took hold and rhythmically began squeezing milk out of his cow, filling the pail about half way.

As Benny and I attacked the food, my father simply watched. "Father, what are you waiting for?" I asked.

"I'm not hungry," he replied.

Benny and I stopped eating, we knew what that meant: He was sacrificing his share for us. We stopped and put the food down.

"If you don't eat, we don't eat!" I firmly stated. The three of us sat there staring at the bounty until my father finally reached down and picked up an egg. We passed the pail of warm milk around, dipping and drinking from an old tin cup.

It didn't matter that there were pieces of black cow manure floating around in the milk. It was just so good!

Dombrovsky sat with us as we ate, asking us about the Germans and the war. My father told him of the German atrocities but left out the part how badly the Polish citizens had been acting. In fact, he made up a story about Polish guards who helped us get away. He didn't want to give Dombrovsky any ideas about collecting rewards.

"Oh, I have to get something from the house Watchmaker. I'll be right back," he said.

The food was all gone when we heard Dombrovsky arguing with his wife in the house. We couldn't understand what she was saying but it was pretty clear it was about us.

The farmer returned with a jar of liquor and two small glasses.

"I made this myself, Watchmaker. Let's have a *schnips*!" he rejoiced.

"You mean a *schnaps*, my friend!" laughed my father.

The two men drank as Benny and I finished the last few sips of milk.

No one wanted to ask why his wife was upset but when the jar was empty and Dombrovsky was drunk, he told us.

"My bitch wife is angry that I gave you our food! I told her that you were the generous Jew that put shoes on our daughters' feet and provided medicine for her sickness, so she shut up! You were good to me that day and giving you a meal is the least I can do."

My father glanced at me. I well understood the precept that from generosity comes generosity.

"But I'm sorry, my friend. Tomorrow night you and your boys have to leave. If the Germans find you here, they will kill us all."

My father understood that Dombrovsky was taking on an overwhelming risk. For helping Jews, his whole family could be slaughtered.

He thanked Dombrovsky profusely before he returned to his house.

My father asked me where we hid the guns. He told us to get them. Then we made a place to sleep in the dusty hayloft of the barn.

For the first time in days, we rested peacefully-- sort of.

The following morning, after the sun came up, we heard the voices of Dombrovsky's family as they began their daily chores. Chickens clucked as they laid their eggs. Other animals stirred in anticipation of their morning meals.

No one except for Dombrovsky and his wife knew that we were in the loft. We watched his daughters, from cracks in the barn walls, as they worked. By now the girls were much older than they were when he came to see us at our shop. They appeared to be ten to fifteen years of age.

They were working together but constantly bickering and throwing insults at each other. They were poorly dressed in patched up dresses and stained aprons. However they did have shoes.

Dombrovsky's wife and his three daughters were hardly attractive, but he was lucky to have them, unlike us who lost all our loved ones.

We watched them carry on their day as we sat quietly up in the loft.

Dombrovsky brought us some more soft-boiled eggs. He reminded us not to get too comfortable, because we had to leave that night.

"Maybe we should go now. I don't trust this Polish farmer!" whispered Benny.

***

My father peeked through the gaps of the dilapidated barn wall and his eyes widened! "There is a Nazi staff car and box truck quickly coming up the road!" he exclaimed.

"I told you these people could not be trusted!" insisted Benny.

It was too late to run. We would be mowed down, trying to get across the meadow to the woods. The Germans pulled off the road and drove down the short driveway into the farm.

"Get your guns ready and find a place to shoot from!" ordered my father.

We quickly gathered our machine guns and braced ourselves for a fight. My father and I stayed in the hayloft as Benny scurried down to the main floor, watching from an open window.

"Don't shoot unless I shoot first, boys," ordered my father. The long black car had Nazi flags and Nazi regalia plastered all over it. The convertible top was down. Actually it looked more like a truck than a car.

It was obvious these were not just any regular German soldiers. They were high level Gestapo SS.

The car came to an abrupt halt. Two Gestapo officers dressed in black exited the vehicle. One was the driver and the other was a black-haired Captain, who seemed to be in charge. The other two soldiers, carrying rifles, also got out of the truck. Dombrovsky left his house and approached the men.

The Captain began shouting and asking him questions. "We're looking for three Jews-- a man with two teenage boys. Have you seen them?"

"No, no I have not seen any Jews around here," replied Dombrovsky.

My father immediately recognized the black-haired Captain!

"He was with Wolfie the night they raided our shop! He was the son of a bitch who beat your mother as they forced her and Hanna onto the truck to the woods," whispered my father.

The Captain became stern and asked why Dombrovsky had not turned over his livestock to the German tax collectors. Dombrovsky explained that without his animals, his family would starve.

"Without your animals I will starve too!" the Captain replied.

He turned and ordered the other soldiers to confiscate all of the livestock.

The three large Germans began heading to the barn, Dombrovsky tried to stop them. One of the soldiers knocked him down and the driver put a gun to his head. His wife and daughters burst out of the house, screaming and running to his aid.

"Take these three young girls too. We will make good use of them tonight!" laughed the Captain.

The men dragged the three girls to the back of the truck and locked them inside. Dombrovsky fell to the Captain's feet. "Sir, those are innocent children. I beg you to leave them with me. My youngest daughter is only ten years old!" he cried.

"You can have them back when I'm done with them! They will be women, not girls, when we are finished with them!" he jeered.

Then he kicked Dombrovsky and laughed.

"Go get the animals!" he barked at his men.

"Wait, wait, sir," exclaimed Dombrovsky. "I have something of interest to you. Maybe you will change your mind, and you will let my girls go free and let me keep my animals!" The Captain became intrigued and paused.

"I'm waiting," yawned the Captain.

We began to panic. We thought we knew what Dombrovsky was going to tell the Captain.

"Get ready boys!" whispered my father.

"Captain, behind the barn near the manure pit. I have a buried treasure of gold coins. My brother stole them from the Jews in Warsaw. He brought it to me to hide for him. But it is buried very deep and my back is broken. I would need some help digging it up," he pleaded.

"Please give me your word that you will leave us alone and I will show you where to dig," he stated.

The Captain instantly agreed and asked to see the location. He ordered the soldiers to get shovels from the truck and they followed the farmer behind the barn.

The area was soaked with animal urine and cow dung. It was a slippery and heavy mess. "Dig here!" Dombrovsky ordered. The three soldiers began digging. After about an hour of laborious digging, the Captain was becoming impatient.

"How much deeper!" he shouted.

"Be patient, my Herr. You will be as rich as a king after we find the box! Remember our deal: You will let my children go and leave my animals," replied Dombrovsky.

"*Ja, Ja.* Let them go, blah, blah, blah," replied the Captain sarcastically.

Suddenly we realized what Dombrovsky was doing: Letting them dig their own grave!

By now the hole was about six feet deep.

"Okay good, I think that's deep enough!" shouted Dombrovsky.

We had maneuvered ourselves down near Benny and watched from a broken window.

"I have to get a long steel rod to poke around," said Dombrovsky. He left the Captain and his soldiers waiting impatiently while he entered the barn.

"Captain, are we really going to leave the girls?" the driver frantically asked.

"Of course not, Dum koph! After we get the gold, we will kill this farmer and his wife and throw them into this hole!" he laughed.

Dombrovsky saw us waiting in the barn with our guns ready. He winked as he walked through the barn. The men were right outside the door. We could hear them complaining about the smell.

"Hey farmer, where are you?!" the Captain shouted.

Tired of waiting, he sent one of his men into the barn. Benny quickly grabbed him from behind, and with his *chalaf*, he cleanly cut his throat from ear to ear. He was dead before he knew what had happened to him.

Then we casually marched out of the barn with our guns raised and confronted the Germans.

"Looking for us, comrades?" my father teased.

The Germans were caught off guard and unarmed, except for the Captain, who was carrying a pistol in his holster. He ordered his men to attack us, but Benny and I quickly shot them to pieces as my father kept his gun trained on the Captain. He cringed in anguish as we mowed down his men. He too was now helpless.

"The night you raided our watch shop, Wolfie sent us to the ghetto, but you beat my wife very badly. You forced her and my little girl onto a truck. Then you took them to the 'Woods,'" my father calmly spoke.

"What happened to my wife and child?" he demanded.

"Go screw yourself, Jew!" the Captain smirked. He then tried to quickly draw his pistol but my father effortlessly shot him in the stomach twice. The man buckled over and fell to the ground. He laid on his back, gasping and holding his belly. My father went over to him and cradled him in his arms.

"I'm not going to screw around with you, ass hole. I'll ask you again. Do you know where my wife and little girl are?" my father scolded.

The Captain's eyes widened as he began coughing up blood.

"*Leck mich am arsch!*" he groaned. Thereupon, my father slapped him hard across the face!

"Where is my wife and child?" he repeated, clenching his teeth.

"You will see them in hell, Watchmaker!" the Captain grunted.

"Before I kill you, you will tell me what I want to know," my father insisted. With his left hand he clenched the Captain's jet-black hair, keeping his head from moving. With his right pointer finger he pushed into the corner of his eye socket and slowly began prying his eyeball out of its socket!

The man screamed in agony as he tried to roll away, but my father motioned to Benny to fall on him and keep him in place. My father continued to dig out his eyeball until it was completely out of his head!

He clenched it tightly in his hand by the cord that was attached to it. The Captain continued to shriek as my father tugged on it!

"I'll give you one more chance before I rip your eyeball out of your skull, you son of a bitch!" shouted my father. The Captain became semi unconscious from the pain, but my father slapped him hard again. Then he started talking.

"We took them to the woods, but it was late, and the killing was stopped for the night. We brought her into the barracks, and we used her over and over, all night like a cheap whore," he smirked and coughed.

"And where was my daughter?" my father shouted. When the Captain hesitated, he gave the eye another tug! He let out another shriek!

"She was on a chair with a sack over her head. We told your woman if she didn't do everything we wanted, we would use the kid instead," the Captain groaned.

"Where are they now!" my father demanded as he shook the dying man.

"Death march to Treblinka, to the extermination camp," he uttered as he winced in pain!

My father looked at us gravely. We were sickened by the sight of my father holding the still-attached eyeball in his fist. With a snap of his elbow, he tore it completely out and threw it to the pigs.

The Captain's scream was like nothing we had ever heard! My father motioned to Benny and said, "Short and sharp!"

He let go of the black hair and used the Captains head to balance as he got up.

Benny removed his *chalaf* from his sheath and sliced through his throat. "Now he is kosher," my father said quietly.

Dombrovsky, who had released his daughters from the truck, had been peeking from inside the barn. When he saw all the Germans were dead, he came out. "Now I have to thank you again, Watchmaker! You saved my daughters and my animals from those bastards."

My father replied, "We thought you were going to turn us in to save your daughters."

"I knew those Nazi bastards would never let us live, if they found you here," said Dombrovsky. "And, I had nothing to offer them but a story of riches. Also, I knew you had guns and would help us. But now I think it would be better for all of us, if you and your boys stay here on the farm."

"Thank you, my friend, but we have something important we have to do. Find my wife and daughter," my father stated. Dombrovsky understood and nodded his head. "First, let's strip the uniforms from these bastards and throw their bodies into the pit. Dombrovsky, can your wife and daughters wash the uniforms and alter them to fit us?" questioned my father. "They will look like new when they are done with them, and they will fit like a glove!" he replied.

"Okay, let's fill the grave and get the car and truck out of sight," father continued..

"Father, what are we going to do?" I questioned.

"We are going to Treblinka to rescue your mother and baby sister," he said with determination.

"We just enlisted into the SS," he joked.

"Dressed as Gestapo? They will never believe I'm an officer. I'm only twelve!" I cried.

"Listen to me son, we have no choice and you are not a boy anymore.

It will be dark, you and Benny will be in the back seat and we are going to be moving fast. No one will expect us to be anything but German scum."

"What is a death march?" Benny asked. Usually he never questioned anything. He was always ready to fight. Maybe it was his anger at the Nazis or maybe just a desire to die and be with his family. Whatever the reason, he was a lot stronger than me.

"They must be forcing people to walk to Treblinka, instead of driving them in trucks. If anyone makes it there alive, they will be murdered for sure," said my father.

***

The Dombrovsky women worked most of the day cleaning and sewing the uniforms. By nightfall they were perfectly cleaned, pressed and altered.

We were able to wash up with soap. My father shaved off his beard but left a strip of a mustache under his nose, a sort of a Hitler mustache. It was shocking to see him this way, but it really did make him look like a Nazi.

The daughters gave us haircuts and greased down our hair to resemble the Germans, and my father practiced the German language Wolfie had taught him. It was similar in many ways to our own language of Yiddish.

"We will leave tonight after supper. I know the way to Treblinka. We should be able to get there in a few hours, God willing," said my father.

Dombrovsky killed a fat chicken. Then we ate what might be our last meal.

We put on the uniforms. It was scary how authentic we looked. Benny was marching around like a Nazi. I had to keep reminding myself that it was Benny and not to shoot him!

"If you want to look like a real Nazi, you have to walk like you have a stick up your ass," Benny joked. We loaded up the car with our things and put up the convertible top.

Dombrovsky filled the staff car's gas tank with gas from the truck and we were ready to go.

My father gave Dombrovsky a few gold coins and a rifle as I climbed into the back seat with Benny.

They briefly discussed a plan that Dombrovsky should follow us with the truck and dump it into the woods a safe distance from his home.

"You know, Watchmaker, I don't even know your name," the farmer stated.

My father smiled and replied, "Joseph".

"Good luck, Joseph," said Dombrovsky and they firmly shook hands.

As he got into the car, my father put on his Gestapo hat. "Short and sharp! Right, Benny!" he said as he started the car. Grinding the gears, he accustomed himself to the vehicle. We slowly pulled out of the driveway and headed west, with Dombrovsky following behind us.

After about thirty minutes, we saw Dombrovsky drive off the road into the woods.

We were on our own. We sped down dirt roads, passing several German encampments. My father was focused. He was determined to find my mother and sister-- or die trying.

We were heading towards Treblinka until we were stopped at a roadblock. A young German soldier approached our car. When he saw what he assumed to be a Gestapo officer in the driver's seat, he immediately came to attention.

"How far is it to Treblinka?" father barked.

"Ten kilometers, sir," the soldier replied.

Our hearts pounded as other soldiers came to investigate.

"What are you waiting for *shiest kopf*! Open the gate I have business to attend to!" shouted my father.

"Sir, they are marching Jews down this road. It may slow you down. Maybe you should take a different route. It would be faster," the man suggested.

"What do I care about Jews?" shouted my father. "I will run them over like cockroaches if they are in my way. Now open the gate! *Schnell*!!"

The guard opened the gate and we quickly accelerated through.

"You make a believable Nazi!" chuckled Benny.

"It was easy. All I had to do is act as if I had a stick up my ass, right Benny!" my father chuckled.

As we drove, I noticed an airstrip in the middle of a large open field. There were dozens of fighter and cargo planes preparing to fuel up from a large inventory of gasoline barrels, which were stacked all around. Many soldiers guarded the area. A large panzer tank sat idle with its turret open.

We were getting close to Treblinka, but had not seen any death march.

After we had traveled about nine kilometers, we noticed bright lights in the distance: Search lights crisscrossing in the darkness.

The road was lined with hundreds of beautiful chestnut trees. How could a place that looked so peaceful, be so evil? I thought.

We drove on but found no marching Jews.

We feared the worst-- that we were too late and that they were already dead. My father sped up and was approaching the exterior of the compound.

We suddenly heard a loud blast from a steam train whistle and saw a long train of about 60 dilapidated wooden cattle cars. It was sitting idle in front of the death encampment, with its large steam engine gently puffing out smoke, and it would occasionally release a blast of hot steam from its massive iron wheels.

"This is Treblinka, the death factory," my father grieved.

We hadn't imagined how big it was! Electric barbed wire encompassed the perimeter and watchtowers with large spotlights overlooked the encampment. SS guards were patrolling with their vicious dogs outside the perimeter of the fencing, itching to kill.

My father drove past the train's steam engine and turned the car around. Some guards noticed us but kept on patrolling since it wasn't unusual for Nazi's to be driving around the area.

I looked over at my father and I could see he was upset by what we were witnessing.

"We have to do something to stop this train!" my father exclaimed.

He stopped the car next to the massive engine. We saw two German SS guards sitting inside the engine compartment, drinking from a large bottle of liquor as they were preparing to leave and pick up another load of Jews for the slaughter.

"Benny, Short and sharp! Let's go!" my father ordered.

"What about me! I'm not staying here alone," I exclaimed.

My father reached into his pocket and handed me his lighter.

Start a fire in the *second* boxcar, then get your ass back into the car!" he ordered.

"The second boxcar? Why not the first one?" I paused to inquire.

"Yes, the second boxcar, you'll understand why when the time comes!" he replied.

We all jumped out of the car and I headed to the open doorway of the second box car, while my father and Benny raced up the ladder that went up to the train's engineer compartment.

The two SS soldiers were surprised when my father and Benny, appearing to be high ranking SS officers, entered their compartment and they immediately dropped their bottle and stood at attention.

"Get off the train! There are Jews hiding in the first boxcar! Get in there and find them, now!" my father shouted.

The men fell over themselves rushing to get off the engine, and they ran to the box car as fast as possible.

I had just stuck my head into the opening of the second boxcar when the stench overwhelmed me!

The boxcars floor was covered with compressed hay, mixed with urine, feces and vomit everywhere!

As I gazed into the inside of the box car. Its interior walls were covered with names, religious prayers and poems that people had scribbled on them.

I noticed a little girl's shoe near the doorway, and it reminded me of my little sister's slipper and the poem I wrote on the wall of our hidden room.

The horrific scenes that these walls have witnessed are now empty and silent, how can this possibly be happening to us!?

I quickly lit my father's lighter, and placed its flame into the hay in the doorway. It flared up and quickly caught fire!

Just then I noticed the two SS guards jumping off the engine and scurrying to the first boxcar, and they quickly climbed inside!

As I rushed over, I understood my father's reasoning and pushed the sliding door closed and locked them inside!

I then ran over to the side of the engine compartment and I saw Benny shoveling coal into the large furnace of the engine and my father was going over the controls.

"Come on, let's get out of here!" I shouted.

Benny threw the shovel down and jumped off the train as my father pushed the accelerator lever forward, and the train began to blast hot steam from its large iron wheels, and it slowly began to chug forward.

As the train began to accelerate, my father pushed the lever to full steam ahead and he jumped off rolling as he hit the ground.

The moving train caught the attention of some of the guards, but they didn't seem to care as long as they didn't have to deal with unloading it.

The train began to quickly pull away and we could vaguely hear the two SS guards kicking at the door and screaming for help, but the roar of the engine's boiler drowned out their cries.

We scampered back into the car and quickly accelerated back the way we came, watching the train catch fire as it sped down the tracks!

"Here's you lighter back Papa, thanks for trusting me to start the fire," I confidently stated. And he reached over his shoulder and took it from me.

"I just want to tell both of you that I'm really proud of you boys, I know I've been hard on you two, but we have to be razor sharp to make it out of here," my father stated.

"Short and sharp," replied Benny

The train was quickly disappearing into the darkness, however we could see that the train was ablaze and burning out of control as the flames were spreading backwards, igniting all the other boxcars as the wind fanned the flames!

A few minutes later we heard a massive explosion in the distance and the black sky lit up red.

"That train will no longer commit its dastardly deeds," my father stated.

And we continued on our quest for my mother and Hanna.

***

"They couldn't have made it this far on foot," my father said. He accelerated the car and we headed back a few kilometers. That's when my father noticed the cigarettes glowing in a harvested potato field.

"This has to be them! Hold on we're going in! Get ready to act like you have a stick up your asses!" commanded my father.

Benny gave me a few nudges with his elbow, and it got my attention. But I was sick with fear. All I could hear was that familiar watch sound beginning to tick in my head.

It was pitch dark as we drove into the potato field. Our headlights lit up the area as we bounced on the rough terrain. There were approximately a hundred men, women and children sleeping on the freshly tilled dirt. About twelve armed guards with several dogs supervised them.

Before any guard could approach us, my father jumped out of the staff car.

"Who is in charge here!?" he shouted.

A sergeant came stumbling over tripping over the dead potato plants. He came to attention when he saw the Gestapo uniform and Captain insignia on the lapel.

"Why has it taken you so long to arrive at the extermination camp? You are an incompetent stooge! What is your name?" he barked.

"Wexler is my name. Sir, we are...are," he stammered, while holding his cigarette.

"Silence! How dare you smoke when addressing a Superior Gestapo officer!" shouted my father. He grabbed the sergeant's hand and buried the lit cigarette into the side of the man's nose! The soldier stood paralyzed, absorbed the pain, as my father extinguished the cigarette.

Some of the other guards drifted over to see what was going on. The dogs were barking wildly out of control.

"Shut up those dogs! Tie them to your truck so I can have some silence! The noise is hurting my ears!" my father shouted. As he covered his ears! The guards quickly gathered the animals and tied them down.

"Sergeant call your men to attention for an inspection immediately. I need to find out who is to blame for your incompetence!" ordered my father.

"Captain, I can assure you that the lateness was not our fault. These lazy Jew bastards were constantly trying to escape. We had to constantly stop and chase them," he exclaimed.

"So these lazy Jews tried to escape! Why didn't you just shoot them? Get everyone up and put them in rows. We are going to execute them right here in the field. *Schnell!*" my father ordered. By this point, he was really into character.

The guards began kicking and beating the prisoners, forcing them to their feet. Dazed and confused, they slowly got up and huddled together.

The light beam from our car dimly lit up the area, as my father desperately searched through the crowd, trying to catch a glimpse of Mother and Hanna.

The people were staggering about in a state of shock and confusion. Having had no food or water for days, they were mentally diminished.

"Hurry up! Quickly!" shouted my father.

Benny and I got out of the car, holding our machine guns, and waited in the dimly lit background. The prisoners were panicking from the commotion, and staggering about so as not to be in the front line.

It was then when my father caught a glimpse of a woman clinging to a little girl. Was it Hanna and my mother?

"Sergeant put your men in line and prepare to shoot these escaping prisoners!" ordered my father.

The prisoners all clung together, some crying, some screaming, anticipating their immediate death as the guards lifted and aimed their rifles.

The ticking in my head began to slow down time. Benny and I positioned ourselves behind my father, as if to take aim at the prisoners.

"Wait one moment! Lower your guns! It sickens me when I have to hear all the loud shrieks and cries of dying Jews. I want to get my ear plugs from the car!" my father shouted.

He turned to us and whispered, "Short and sharp!"

Tick. Tick. Tick. Tick. Tick.

Time began to stand still, as Benny and I squeezed our triggers, firing away! Our guns cranked out bullets and we filled the guards with bullets!

Their dogs barked ferociously, trying to break free from their ties.

The Germans seemed to fall in slow motion. Some squeezed off shots but were finished off quickly as we filled their bodies with more hot lead.

My father ran into the crowd of prisoners, searching for Mother and Hanna. Frantically he juggled people to see their faces, but they were frightened and turned away. For several moments, he disappeared into the chaotic crowd.

But, then he emerged from the chaos, miraculously clutching Hanna, while Mother attacked him and fought to get her baby back from him. She was relentless--not realizing it was her husband who had come to save her. She was fighting him for Hanna!

I quickly grabbed Hanna and put her into the car.

My mother was still ferociously fighting, trying to get Hanna back.

"It's me Joseph! Your husband!" my father shouted. He shook her and slapped her. Finally she realized who he was and that we were there to rescue them. They were safe now. She softened her stance and deeply embraced and kissed her husband.

"I thought you were dead!" cried my father.

She stood poised and dignified as they embraced. "I am dead, always tell the children I loved them so much," she whispered.

The slow ticking in my head continued as she reached down and pulled his pistol out from his holster and pointed it to her head. Before my father could stop her, she pulled the trigger.

"Nooooo. Nooooo!!" my father hysterically cried.

The loud bang of the gun sent the crowd into a frenzy. They pushed and shoved, trying to get past my father. He tightened his grip on my mother, as she became limp. He wailed uncontrollably.

In the chaos Benny shouted to the prisoners. "*Landsmen*...we are here to rescue you. Take the guards' guns and run to the woods and hide. Break up into smaller groups and head east to Russia."

My father refused to let my mother go. She killed herself because she could never overcome that horrific night she spent with the German men. It was only to protect Hanna that she did what she had to do. Now she was at peace with herself. In her heart, she regained her dignity and honor.

Benny shouted to my father that we had better leave. The Jewish prisoners were slaughtering the dogs with the clubs they took from the dead guards.

"They could turn on us. Let's go!" shouted Benny

Father kissed our mother one last time and laid her carefully on the ground. I held Hanna closely and cried in the back seat of the car, but Hanna was in a trance -like state: just sitting next to me as if she was somewhere else.

My father and Benny raced back to the car. He started the car and Benny jumped into the front passenger seat, looking over his shoulder at Hanna and me. "Are you okay, Hanna?" he asked. She made no response and just sat there in a daze.

My father was fighting back his tears as we sped away. He was trying to get his composure back. The shoulder on his uniform was stained with my mother's blood. I placed my hand on it. That was all we had left of her.

After driving only a few hundred yards down the road, he abruptly pulled over and jumped out of the car. He quickly opened the back door and grabbed hold of Hanna. He held her tightly, as if he was never going to let her go again. He could feel her breath and her warm skin as he caressed her soiled hair.

He began to realize that something was wrong with her, as she was unresponsive. He loosened his hold and looked into her eyes. There was nothing there but a cold motionless stare.

"Hanna, I'm your father and this is your brother Jacob," he said softly.

"You know Benny, your brother's best friend." Benny took his hat off and made a funny face, but there was no response. She was in a state of shock.

Father placed her carefully back in the seat and slowly released his hold.

"What's wrong with her?" I asked.

"She went through a lot for a six-year-old, Koby. She saw and heard things that a child should never have to experience." He didn't say any more, but we both knew he was referring to the fact that she was in the room when they were raping mother. And she had also seen innocent people viciously murdered by the Germans.

"We have to give her some time," he said. He closed the door and went back to the driver's seat. We sped off back the way we came. As I sat quietly with Hanna I thought, where is our God now?

***

"What are we going to do now? Are we going back to the farm?" Benny asked.

"No, we are going to that airfield we passed, and we are going to commandeer a plane out of here?" my father stated.

"How are we going to fly a plane? None of us has ever even been in one! Let's keep driving south, like we originally planned!" I pleaded.

But father countered my pleas.

"We have no choice. The fastest way out of here is to fly. You have to stop arguing with me, Koby. You have been against every plan I've come up with. We made it this far, you have to show some confidence in me!" he exclaimed.

"Ok, Papa, I'm sorry, but I'm really scared!" I replied.

We drove for several kilometers until we saw the lighted area of the airfield. My father stopped the car and asked Benny to go to the car's trunk and get our old clothes. Benny grabbed the clothes and noticed an extra rucksack with ammunition, which he threw over his shoulder. And he tossed the garments onto Koby in the back seat.

"Jacob, hide Hanna on the floor and cover her up with our clothes," he ordered.

I placed Hanna on the floor. She made no effort to resist.

I carefully covered her, concealing her from sight.

My father started the car and we sped off. The airfield was in sight. The area was brightly lit and there were hundreds of barrels of gasoline stacked high, all around the airfield. We saw dozens of men, mostly laborers, loading supplies while some soldiers marched around the perimeter.

There was one gravel runway with several transport planes lining up for takeoff as we approached the main gate.

"I have an idea!" my father exclaimed. He turned to Benny.

"Buckle over and hold your belly. Pretend you are unconscious. Koby, make sure the safety switch on your gun is on red, and be ready to fight for our lives!"

He accelerated the car and screeched to a stop when we arrived at the gate. Two infantry guards came running with their guns raised and pointing at the car.

"Idiots, put your guns down! Can't you see we are Gestapo!?" shouted my father. The guards quickly lowered their weapons and came to attention.

"I have an injured soldier here! This is Heimlich Himmler's nephew!" he continued. We need a doctor *schnell*! The guards opened the gate. One spoke.

"There is no doctor here, but go in. I will call the commandant. He will know what to do!" he said.

My father quickly accelerated through the gate and drove into the airfield. We were met by a Captain, who was quickly trying to dress and put his boots on, as he stumbled out of his barracks. He raced over to our car.

"This is Heimlich Himmler's nephew. We were attacked by a group of partisans!" my father shouted.

The Captain saw the blood on my father's shoulder. Benny was moaning while holding his belly.

"There is no doctor here, but we can put you on a plane to Berlin right away!" he stated.

"If this man dies, I can assure you that we will all go to the Russian front!" my father retorted.

"Drive your car and park next to the air strip," said the Captain.

He ran alongside our car and told us to stop just on the grass next to a cargo plane that was taxiing on the runway. The captain motioned to the pilot to stop and ordered him to wait.

The pilot opened his window. The Captain told him there was an emergency. He was to take Himmler's nephew to Berlin for medical attention.

The pilot turned to his copilot, telling him to go back and he opened the plane's heavy door. My father and I quickly got out of the car.

Frantically we lifted Benny out of the car and dragged him towards the plane, leaving our guns behind. Suddenly we noticed three tall men marching down the plane's steps wearing black Gestapo uniforms. Once again, the ticking began in my head.

"What's going on here? Why are we stopping!" one of the officers shouted.

The captain told them about the situation.

"What kind of bullshit is this? I know Himmler, and he doesn't have a nephew old enough to be in the *Reich*!" shouted the SS officer.

They instantly raised their pistols at us. We froze.

"Who are you?" shouted one of the officers. We stood paralyzed as they took my father's pistol and pushed us away from the car.

They quickly determined we were not Gestapo, and that Benny and I were too young to be soldiers.

They ordered my father to open his coat and shirt, as they checked his body for the telltale tattoo that every SS officer was required to have: a small swastika or blood type below the armpit.

"I think we have found the three Jews everyone has been looking for!" one of them rejoiced.

The officers began kicking and beating us while the plane's engine continued to idle.

"How did you get these Gestapo uniforms and car?" another officer shouted. We refused to talk as they continued to beat us.

"Captain, radio the Major and tell him to come to the airfield. We have a surprise for him. He can deal with these Jews," a senior officer ordered.

We slowly pulled ourselves up from the ground, using the car for balance.

I looked up and saw a shooting star racing across the sky. It was the first time I had ever seen one. It broadly streaked across the sky, disappearing as quickly as it came.

How could such a beautiful thing like that show up now? I thought to myself.

The officers backed away from us. They were standing in front of a tall stack of gasoline barrels with their pistols aimed at us. They motioned us to move away from the car with their guns and we obeyed. Just as the Jews did, who were running up to the top of the trenches at the Willows, before they were assassinated.

Now I understood what they were feeling: an empty hopefulness for mercy that would never come.

The pilot shouted to the officers they were keeping other planes from taking off.

"Let's just kill them now and be done with it! I have to be back for my daughter's birthday party by morning," the senior officer complained.

"But the Major will be angry that we killed his Jews before he gets here!" said another officer.

"The commandant can report that they tried to escape, and we had no choice," the senior officer replied.

"*Ja*, and let's make some sport of them! The person who gets the closest shot between the Jews' eyes, wins a stein of beer at the Haufbrau Haus!" the other SS officer exclaimed.

Tick. Tick. Tick. There it was again, as I drifted into thought about my mother. I remembered the strength, dignity and honor she had exhibited when they took her

"We must stand tall!" I exclaimed.

We stood there in that spirit, as we prepared to die.

The Nazis were laughing, eager to make sport of us. With their backs against the barrels they aimed their pistols at our faces.

Tick. Tick. Tick…Tick……..Tick………..Tick.

My father began reciting a mourner's prayer in Hebrew as he held us by his side for the last time and Benny joined in.

The officers raised their pistols and took careful aim at our heads.

All I could hear was the decelerating ticking in my head and the faint sound of my father repeating his prayers, as we prepared for death.

That slow intermittent ticking in my brain served to reduce my mind into a state of slow motion. Without moving, I gazed down the barrel of the gun. The round black hole seemed to stare back at me, as I awaited its bullet to strike my head.

Time and sound almost ceased to exist as frame-by-frame in slow motion images flashed before my eyes. Our short lives were over.

Then I saw the three officers horrifically surprised as they turned their attention away from us in slow motion. And suddenly I heard the sound of machine gun fire coming from beside us. The officer's bodies shook erratically and then were thrown back against the barrels of fuel. Flesh and blood splattered all around them.

The few seconds seemed to last minutes as I slowly turned my attention toward the car.

There was so much smoke coming from it, I could only see red flames jerking out of a machine gun! The shooting stopped only when the gun was empty.

The three officers lay dead, cut to pieces, in pools of their blood. And fuel leaked over their lifeless bodies.

As the white smoke began to clear, to my astonishment, I saw an angry little girl clutching my machine gun! She had it propped up on the window frame of the car door. Her tiny finger was still holding back the trigger! It was Hanna!!

She began crying, as she released all that trauma which had been pent up inside her tiny body.

My father ran over to her, and pulled her from the car, as Benny gathered our guns and his blade.

I stood there paralyzed in disbelief. "Are we still alive?" I asked myself.

Benny shook me out of my trance and handed me a gun. "Let's go! Short and sharp!" he rejoiced.

Chapter Five

My father carried Hanna and we quickly headed for the airplane.

Benny was first on the stairs, but the co-pilot tried to push him off and close the door.

"Hey, do you want to die, sauerkraut?" I shouted to him.

I pointed my machine gun and motioned for him to jump off. As he jumped, Benny hit him from behind with his gunstock and knocked him unconscious.

My father handed Hanna to Benny and jumped back down the steps, rushing back to the runway. I saw him reach into his pocket for his lighter, as he ran toward the bodies of the dead SS officers. He lit his lighter, and tossed it into the pool of gasoline that had leaked all over their bodies. It flashed into a small explosion and the fire trailed its way back to the stockpiled barrels.

He quickly ran back, and jumped onto the plane, closing the heavy door behind him.

My father then swiftly made his way to the cockpit, where the pilot was sitting.

He noticed pictures of the man's wife and children taped to the instrument panel and his name "Fritz" was written on his helmet.

The pilot, who was strapped into his seat, seemed to be surprised to see my father standing there with a gun.

"Listen...Fritz. I see you have a very lovely family. If you ever want to see them again, I suggest you do what I say. I can kill you right now, or you can cooperate with me and be with your family again," stated my father.

The pilot nodded his head, affirming he would like to choose life.

"Where would you like me to take you, *Herr Zeiger Meister?*" the pilot smiled.

"Get up in the air, *schnell*! We're going to Sweden," ordered my father.

My father kept his gun trained on the pilot, as he climbed into the copilot's seat. The pilot then accelerated the plane's engines and we began to move.

"How do you know who I am?" my father asked.

"The entire SS is searching for you and your boys. You killed many of those Gestapo bastards. It made the SS look very weak, that you were able to do that. Believe me, many in the German army, including myself, hate the Gestapo too. We are happy you killed them!" replied the pilot.

We quickly gained speed and raced down the runway. The plane began to rock as barrels of gasoline began to ignite and exploded behind us!

I looked out the window and saw barrels exploding, and flying through the air hitting one another! It set off a chain reaction, causing the whole airfield to become engulfed in flames! Buildings, airplanes, other equipment-- everything was on fire!

In less than a minute we were airborne. It was an odd feeling. Our ears began popping as our altitude increased. When we leveled off, Benny began rummaging through some of the large wooden crates, that were stored behind us in the cargo area. He used the butt of his gun and managed to knock open a few of them.

"Is there any food back there?" I asked.

He reached into one of the crates and pulled out a handful of tins.

"Good news: Sardines! Hundreds of tins of Sardines...Bad news, we don't have a can opener!" he exclaimed.

He continued rummaging through several other crates, as I sat with Hanna. She clung to me and asked me where Mama was. I didn't have the heart or strength to tell her, so I told her that Papa would tell her later.

As we sat waiting for my father to return, I accidentally kicked something under our seat. I reached down, and found three large leather valises made of black leather. Each had a red swastika embossed on the flap. They seemed very full.

"These must belong to those SS officers," I thought.

"Hey, Benny, come check this out," I said.

He came over, carrying a few bottles of seltzer water, and handed one to each of us.

He picked up a valise and opened the buckles. Inside were scores of papers marked "Top Secret!"

"I can't read it. It's all written in German, but it looks pretty important," he exclaimed.

He continued rummaging through the valise and pulled out several maps.

"Where did you find these cases?" Benny asked.

I pointed under our seat. He bent over and reached to the side, when he took hold of something. It was a fancy box with pink ribbon and a bow tied around it.

Benny ripped it open. A little girl's white and pink party dress fell out of it.

Hanna's eyes widened when she saw it.

"This must be for you, Hanna!" Benny said with a smile. Benny continued looking under the seats as I brought Hanna to the toilet compartment on the plane.

I cleaned her up and removed the heavily soiled clothes that she had been wearing since the Germans had taken her. I helped her slip the new dress on. It fit her perfectly! She ran her hands over it, and I could see that she felt human again.

We returned to our seat and Benny smiled "What a pretty little girl you are Hanna!" he said. She smiled as we sat back down.

"Look what else I found," stated Benny. He was holding a small metal strong box.

It had the royal seal of Poland on the lid, but it was locked.

"What do you think is inside it?" I asked.

"I don't know, but it looks like it came from the Polish treasury. Probably something the Germans stole from the government is my guess," he replied.

Benny had managed to open a few tins of sardines with a pocket knife he had found, and we ate.

My father sat with the pilot until we were airborne, and he made sure that we were on course to Sweden.

"No funny business. You have my word that you can go free when we land. And if you wish, sit out the war in Sweden. I expect to see the compass pointing north," stated my father.

He tore the radio microphone off the radio, and told the pilot that he was going back to check on the passengers.

"I will fly us to Sweden, *Herr Meister*. I do not want to die for Hitler. That maniac is a crazy son of a bitch," the pilot said.

When father arrived at the cargo area, where we were sitting, he was surprised to see Hanna in the new dress, and acting more like his little girl.

"Look at my princess!" he exclaimed.

He took Hanna in his arms and she hugged him tightly.

I handed him a bottle of seltzer and a tin of sardines. "Look what we found under the seats Papa," I said.

His eyebrows lifted when he saw the three valises and the strong box.

"They are all full of 'top secret' files but we don't know what they say, because they are written in German. The strong box is locked but it is not very heavy," Benny said.

"When we get to Sweden we can look into it. For now let's just rest," replied my father.

"Papa, where is Mama?" Hanna asked.

Father paused. "Let's just rest, Hanna. Let's just rest," he said softly.

"Papa," I whispered. "How is it that when the SS officers were shot up, that the fuel barrels behind them did not explode? The bullets only made holes in the barrels."

He explained, "Gasoline needs either a very high temperature or a spark to ignite. The bullets are made of lead, which is too soft to create a spark, when they penetrated the steel barrels. And the air passing over the bullets cooled them enough to lower their temperature."

Suddenly my father realized something:

"Boys, what did you take from the car when we left?" he questioned in alarm.

"I just took the guns and the rucksack full of ammunition that I had on my back," Benny replied.

My father put his hands on his head. "We forgot the sack of gold coins in the trunk!" my father cried. "It will be difficult to get around with no money, but we will figure it out."

He bounced Hanna on his knee. For the first time, I saw her laugh again.

"Koby, check the guns and see how much ammunition is left in Benny's bag," my father said.

I picked up each machine gun. The bullet clips were full, except for the one Hanna had used.

Benny handed me his rucksack. It felt like it was full of ammunition.

I opened the sack, and in the dim light I saw what seemed to be loose bullets in it. I reached in. To my surprise, right on top, was the bell from our store!

"Hey Papa look! It's the bell from the store!" I exclaimed.

"Great, we can use it to beg for money in the streets of Stockholm," he kiddingly replied.

I reached into the bag again. At once I realized it did not contain loose ammunition. Rather it was the bag of gold coins! Benny had taken it from the staff car's trunk!

"Papa, we don't have any more bullets, see for yourself," I complained.

I passed the sack to my father and he carefully reached into the bag. His eyes lit up as he grasped a fistful of golden coins!!

"Oh my, thank you Benny!" my father exclaimed. Benny was puzzled.

"What did I do?" he asked.

"You took the wrong sack which was the right sack!" rejoiced my father.

Father removed two of the gold coins and brought a few tins of sardines to the cockpit.

"Here my friend is a gold coin. When we land safely in Sweden, you will get a second one," my father stated.

He then offered the pilot a tin of sardines. The pilot took the coin and placed it in an ashtray on the instrument panel. He then reached down under his seat and felt around for something.

My father, convinced he was going for a gun, immediately pointed his pistol at the pilot's head!

The pilot froze. Slowly he lifted his hand, revealing a shiny metal object in his grasp. "*Bitte*, I believe we are in need of a can opener, *mein Herr*?" he said.

My father was relieved. He put down the gun and took the can opener.

"*Danke Fritz,*" he chuckled. And he sunk back into the co-pilot's seat and checked the compass. It was pointing northwest.

"How long before we get to Sweden?" my father asked.

"We should be in Swedish air space sometime in the early morning. I'm not sure but I think we have just enough fuel to make it over the sea. However, landing may be difficult since we don't have a radio. They might believe we are attacking them and shoot us down. We'll have to fly in low, below their radar and find an isolated place to land."

"If we're not shot down, what do you plan to do when we get there?" he continued.

"We'll need to get to Stockholm, and get into the American Embassy," my father replied. In turn, he asked the pilot, "What are you going to do, my friend? I can vouch for you that you helped us get away."

The pilot replied, "I'm not so sure about the American Embassy, but I will seek Swedish Asylum and try to sit out the war there. If I go back to Germany, the Gestapo will surely execute me for treason. They will call me a traitor for not doing my duty, for not crashing the plane to kill us all."

My father reached into his pocket and gave the pilot the other gold coin.

"Here, the gold coins should help you get off to a good start. You know Fritz, for a German, you're not such a bad fellow," my father joked.

"Thank you *Herr Zeiger Meister*, and you're not such a bad Jew either!" he retorted.

"I'm going to fly up the eastern coast toward Stockholm, until we start to run out of gas. Hopefully we'll find a place to land."

"Yes, and not get blown out of the sky," said my father.

***

After flying most of the night, the morning finally came, and the sun's beaming ray shining on my face woke me. I looked out the window and saw that we were flying over water.

Father came back to check on us. He reported we would be landing in less than an hour. I could make out the coastline of Sweden in the distance where its land met the sea.

Suddenly our plane erratically jerked and lurched! I could hear faint machine gun fire and bullets hitting our plane as we quickly began to lose altitude!

I scrambled to look out the window. There were two German fighter planes rapidly flying past us! One of our engines was badly smoking and the other stopped altogether! Benny jumped up from his sleep and frantically asked what was happening!

"They must have sent fighter planes to catch up to us! There are no guns on this plane that can shoot them down! We're going to be shot to pieces!" I cried.

My father returned to the cockpit and shouted to stay down! I pushed Hanna to the floor, and she held onto the seat frame. Benny took off back to the cargo area.

"Where are you going Benny?" I shouted.

"I'll be right back!" he replied.

"What are we going to do—throw tins of sardines and spray seltzer at them?" I shouted.

Benny returned dragging two long black wooden boxes. He popped the lid off one of them. In it were two brand new fifty-caliber machine guns! The other box contained numerous belts of ammunition!

"I thought you said there was nothing back there!" I exclaimed.

"I said there was no food back there! Come on let's get these things loaded!"

We quickly loaded a long bandolier of bullets into each of the big guns breeches. The bullets were huge! Each one was capable of doing massive damage.

"We have to smash out the windows, one on each side of the plane!" Benny exclaimed.

Without hesitation, I picked up a machine gun and blasted out the windows glass. We saw the planes circling back for another run at us.

"Get ready, Koby. They don't know it yet, but they are going to get a big surprise!" shouted Benny.

We hoisted our guns to the windows and balanced the underside of the barrels on the base of the window frames.

"These guns are going to kick your ass, if you're not holding them tightly! Make sure you have the butt tight on your shoulder!" Benny shouted.

Meanwhile my father stayed in the cockpit helping the pilot, in case he was hit. He kept calling back to us, but we were too busy to answer.

"Here they come again! They're crossing over us!" Benny shouted.

As I focused on what was happening, my internal "ticking" started in, once again. The planes were getting closer! Given that we had no mounted guns, they thought we were sitting ducks. I could see them firing their guns as they sped toward us.

Then we pulled our triggers! The big guns began chugging out those giant bullets! They banged like sledge hammers against our shoulders! Together, Benny and I filled the sky with enormous lead armaments!

I shot at one of the fighter planes until its engine began to smoke and it veered downward, spiraled away and exploded behind us!

Benny was filling the other fighter plane with holes, until part of its wing broke off and it crossed in front of me. I saw the pilot's horrified face as he frantically tried to regain control of his plane, but the plane began to nose dive and crashed into the sea below!

"Yahoo!" I shouted.

"Short and sharp, you Sons of a bitches!!" Benny roared.

Our own plane began to cough, and we continued to lose altitude. My father came running back to see what all the commotion was about. Hanna jumped up into his arms. "Where did those guns come from?" he asked.

"It's a long story!" Benny chuckled.

"I'm proud of you boys. You did good! But I don't know how much longer this plane can stay up. It's full of holes and the engine is dying.

As soon as we can find a place, we're going to make a hard landing, so hold on," my father stated.

Finally we were over land. Below us, we could see the Swedish landscape. Occasionally we could even see people pointing up at us. We followed the rocky coastline until an area opened up suitable for landing.

My father once again returned to us and sat down with Hanna.

"Okay, he said. There is about a quarter kilometer of open beach in front of us. Brace yourselves. We're going to try to land on the beach."

We heard the engine decelerate. Then the pilot applied the air brakes, and we felt the plane lurch back, slowing down our air speed.

Our injured plane was now bucking up and down and side to side! But we were getting closer and closer to the ground.

At our feet, hundreds of empty shell casings were sliding all around, making a racket. My stomach started to turn over and I felt nauseous. The plane was bucking and moving from side to side.

My sister began throwing up sardines as my father held her.

Benny was turning green, and trying to remain calm!

The closer we dropped to the beach, the faster it seemed we were going!

I glanced out the window and could see waves alongside us! Suddenly the wheels touched wet firm sand. The plane bucked one last time and we actually coasted to a smooth stop!

Benny jumped out of his seat, frantically pushing the aircrafts door open! He vaulted out of the plane and I was right behind him! We fell onto the sandy beach, and we had become violently ill.

My father staggered out too, carrying Hanna. He also collapsed on the beach, and the four of us lay in the sand, vomiting sardines!

"Isn't it great to be alive?" Benny groaned as he heaved.

"Benny, PLEASE, PLEASE KILL ME!" I moaned.

The pilot strutted off the plane carrying a few bottles of seltzer water.

"Here this will make you feel better," he said. "You green horns would never make it in the Luftwaffe!" he joked.

The cool autumn breeze felt good and we began to settle down.

We slowly staggered to our feet, taking in the fresh sea air.

We made it, boys!" my father semi-rejoiced. "Let's get our things and find our way to Stockholm."

Slowly we dragged ourselves back into the plane.

"Do we still need our guns, Papa?" I asked.

"The way things have been going... yes," he replied.

We took the folders out of the SS officer's black valises. Benny noticed a duplicate file containing the names of hundreds of Nazi SS officers. It also had their pictures, rank and places where they were posted.

"I'm going to keep this one for a souvenir," said Benny.

We found several large rucksacks and placed the folders and maps in one of them. In the other sack we placed the strong box, our gold coins, and the bell from the store.

"Take some seltzer bottles, but leave the sardines!" my father said.

As we prepared to leave, suddenly it occurred to us that we were still dressed as SS officers and had no change of clothes.

We're going to scare a lot of people dressed like this. If we run into the Swedish army, they may think we are the enemy," I said.

"We'll try to find new clothes on the way to Stockholm. In the meantime, clean up and continue to act like you have a stick up your ass," said my father.

Carrying our guns and rucksacks, we exited the plane.

Fritz the pilot was outside sitting on the bullet ridden wing, smoking a cigarette.

"I think you should come with us, my friend. You might get picked up by the Swedish military if you stay here and you will have no one to back up your story," stated my father. "But who will guard the sardines?? Thank you, *Herr Zeiger Meister*, but I think I'll take my chances. Good luck to you and your children. I hope you find peace," Fritz replied.

Before we separated, he gave my father a piece of paper with the address of his home in Germany.

"After the war, please send me a letter. I would like to know how you made out," stated the pilot.

***

They shook hands and we parted ways. We began trekking north. The sandy beach quickly turned into a rocky shoreline and it became difficult to walk.

Benny and my father took turns carrying Hanna on their shoulders, since she was too little to keep up with us. We walked for several hours. However, the terrain became extremely difficult and we had to stop.

We sat and rested on some large ocean boulders, when my father noticed a small motorized fishing boat, a few hundred yards out.

"Boys hide behind the rocks!" my father ordered.

We took his guns and hid, as father held Hanna and shouted to the fisherman.

"Help! Help!" he shouted as he held Hanna as high as he could. Hanna was waving her arms shouting too.

The fisherman heard their cries and turned his boat to shore. The sea was rough, but the fisherman maneuvered his boat close to shore. The fisherman could not understand what my father was saying and refused to come closer.

My father put down Hanna, then reached into his rucksack and removed a large gold coin. He held it up for the fisherman to see. The fisherman's eyes opened wide, and he moved his boat closer. He pulled it near the rocky edge, but it was not close enough for father and Hanna to get in.

The man motioned to my father to throw the sack to him first. Then he would come closer. But my father became suspicious and refused.

"You come closer!" my father motioned.

The fisherman now became angry. He reached into a compartment and pulled out an old rusty pistol, aiming it at my father! Once again he motioned to my father to throw the rucksack into the boat and cocked the hammer on his gun!

At that point, my father instead dropped the rucksack on the rocks and picked up Hanna. The fisherman pulled his boat up to shore and dropped anchor. He signaled my father to back away, as he stepped off the boat.

Then he motioned to him to turn around.

When the fisherman indeed found the fortune of gold coins in the sack, he began to get excited and laugh as he ran his greedy fingers through the bounty.

Benny and I watched from behind a large rock.

"You know, I'm really starting to lose faith in humanity," Benny whispered.

"Starting?" I replied.

The fisherman stood up and took aim at the back of my father's head while Hanna clung to him.

My father stood there still, waiting for us to act. "Okay boys! I think now would be a great time to do something!" he said.

The fisherman had no idea what he was saying and thus paid no attention.

Benny and I chambered bullets into our machine guns and wandered out from behind the rocks, shooting a rip of bullets into the air. The fisherman froze as he saw he was outnumbered and more so, out gunned.

My father turned around and harshly took the pistol away from the fisherman. He threw it into the sea as Benny and I kept our guns trained on him.

"What about that big knife he has on his belt, Papa?" I questioned.

"I don't think he is going to throw it at us," he replied.

The fisherman stood there, staring at the ground, unable to look us in the eyes.

"What are we going to do with this piece of shit?" Benny asked.

My father took my gun. He told us to take Hanna and the rucksacks and get into the boat.

My father then ordered the fisherman to "Go!" and he pointed back from the direction we came. The man was confused, so my father pushed him with his gun and pointed firmly. The man slowly began to walk away, peering over his shoulder occasionally as if to ward off being shot in the back.

"Run, run away!" my father shouted. He fired some shots near the feet of the fisherman, and he took off! As he ran away, he tripped and stumbled over rocks. But he was finally gone.

We all got into the boat. Benny pulled up the anchor. My father took the steering wheel and accelerated the gas lever and away we went, following the coastline north.

"I would have given that guy the 'Short and Sharp!'" Benny exclaimed.

"If we weren't there, he would have killed you, Papa!" I added.

"I don't think he could have pulled the trigger. It's not easy to kill someone if you've never done it before. Besides we did enough killing," he said.

"How do you know he never killed anyone before?" Benny questioned.

My father thought for a moment "Damm, you are right! We should go back and hunt that bastard down!" he chuckled.

After traveling for about an hour, we saw a group of boats tied to a dock in the distance. As we approached we could see a small coastal village. We drove up to the docks and tied off the boat.

"Let's go see where we are," said my father.

Reluctantly we threw our machine guns into the sea. All we had left was my father's pistol, which he hid in his rucksack.

As we walked down the dock, we saw fishermen returning with their catches and sea birds circling around them. The smell of fish sickened us, and we quickly left the area.

We walked down a main street and found an old man walking a small dog. *"Sprechen sie Deutsch?"* my father asked, still in German character. The man didn't understand at all but motioned us to keep heading down the road.

We continued to a marketplace. There were scores of people there, shopping and carrying on. It was odd to see so many blond-haired men and women in one place. Suddenly my father shouted at the top of his lungs! *"Das Deutsch sprechen Sich?"* He was hoping someone would speak German and direct us to the American Embassy.

"Ja wir sprechen Deutsch!" shouted a man in the distance. We could see people moving through the crowd as someone was coming towards us.

The crowd broke open. We were stunned when a group German SS officers were now standing before us!

A Nazi Captain stood face to face with my father, gazing at him!

"You are coming with us!" he ordered.

The other officers drew their weapons, and pointed them at us.

"These men are guilty!" shouted the Captain.

We had come so far and were on the brink of freedom and now this!

"These men are guilty! Of having no beer in their fists!" the Captain shouted, and the men roared with laughter.

At once we realized they were all totally drunk from having consumed beer all day. Recklessly they put their weapons down. The Captain slapped my father on the back!

"Join us, friend! We are going to the pub to celebrate our time off from killing Jews at Auschwitz! You are coming with us!" stammered the drunken SS officer.

He took my father's rucksack, which contained the gold coins, strong box and the only weapon we had, and swung it onto his shoulder.

"What do you have in here? Gold!" he joked. And they all laughed.

The men began pushing us towards the pub across the street. Father edged me aside with Hanna.

"Go find us a ride out of here. We will be out as soon as we can," he whispered.

Hanna and I blended into the crowd as I watched Benny and my father enter the pub with the Germans.

"Beer for everyone!" a lieutenant shouted to the bartender.

He quickly served up steins of beer and served them to the men.

Benny asked the bartender where the toilet was. He was directed to the back of the pub. As Benny went there, he passed a storage room. It contained a sink, empty liquor bottles and all sorts of other supplies for the pub.

On the floor Benny noticed a large amber glass bottle with a white label attached to it. It read "POISON" and there was a drawing of an upside down dead rat printed on it. "Rat Poison," Benny whispered to himself.

Benny carefully poured the liquid into an empty liquor bottle. In another bottle he poured water from the sink.

Upon his return to the bar area, he shouted, "Another round of beer on me!!". The men cheered as the bartender set them up.

"A toast to Hitler!" Benny proclaimed.

The men cheered as they held up their steins and drank. My father had no idea what Benny was up to, but he casually removed his rucksack off the Captain's shoulder. "To Deutschland!" Benny shouted as he revealed the two bottles of liquor.

He began pouring the water from the first bottle into his cup and the remaining into father's. He then opened the second bottle and began pouring large amounts of the liquid poison into the steins of the eager SS Officers.

"To the Gestapo!" Benny shouted. The men cheered wildly and drank their entire steins, as Benny pretended to drink the bitter brew.

"Another round!" Benny insisted. The bartender quickly served another round. The men took a long quick gulps to make room for their second liquor shot.

Again Benny poured a larger quantity of the poison into the men's steins. They were so drunk they didn't realize that he had skipped his own stein and that of father's.

Benny lifted his glass, shouting, "Kill the *Juden*!" The men roared! Cheering and wildly screaming, they drank to the bottom. Meanwhile Benny and father returned their steins full to the bar.

"Benny, what's going on?" my father asked.

"Short and sharp, Rat poison," replied Benny.

The officers continued to carry on as Benny and my father excused themselves.

"Good day gentlemen, we have a plane to catch back to Poland. Lots of *Juden* to catch, you know," sarcastically stated my father. Suddenly one of the men started to grimace and buckled over.

Then, one by one, the other SS officers did the same. Blood began pouring from their eyes, ears and nostrils as the poison took hold. They began insanely thrashing about the pub knocking over chairs and smashing into the tables!

The pub emptied, as patrons scrambled to get out. Benny and my father stood in the doorway and watched as one of the officers beat his head against the bar, cracking his skull open.

Another officer repeatedly banged his head against the wall and began biting his fingers off! Yet another one began clubbing himself to death with the leg of a table then began tearing out chunks of his hair! It was grueling to witness, and it wasn't over until their seizures finally ended and they were dead.

"I could have put them out of their misery with a bullet. But they are miserable Nazis and they deserved a miserable death," my father stated. And they quickly left the pub.

Chapter Six

I was waiting in the marketplace with Hanna, when Benny and my father came running towards us.

"What did you find out, Koby," my father questioned. "There's a bus that leaves for Stockholm every morning at eight o'clock. The bus stop is right around the corner," I reported.

"Okay, we'll have to spend the night here and catch the morning bus," father said. He looked around and saw several policemen rushing toward the pub. "We need to get out of this area before someone recognizes us."

We went down an alley and up several cross streets. It was late afternoon. We didn't even know what day it was. We finally came across a stretch of stores in a main square. There was even a bank and a hotel in the plaza.

My father took off his rucksack and removed a few gold coins.

"I'm going into the bank to turn these into Swedish money. I'll be right back," he said. A few minutes later he returned.

"Let's go shopping," he chuckled.

There were all sorts of clothing stores in the square. We spent the rest of the afternoon buying new clothes and food from street vendors.

Benny wanted to keep his uniform as a souvenir, and he stuffed it into his sack.

When we entered a shoe store, I couldn't help but to think about Dombrovsky. How a chance encounter with a farmer looking to sell some butter, would later help us survive and save Hanna from death. It was remarkable.

As we walked freely down the streets, we began to feel human again.

We entered the hotel and father got us two adjoining rooms. We each took our time bathing. My father finally shaved off his hideous "Hitler mustache." It felt so good to feel clean again. Later we all went downstairs to the dining room. A waiter sat us down at a large table.

The man, who spoke a little Polish, asked Benny what he would like.

"I'll eat anything, just please don't bring me any fish!" he replied.

We all laughed, but the waiter didn't understand what was so funny. We ate like royalty that night. No matter what the cost, we earned it. After we finished our desserts we retired to our rooms.

"Let's open up the strong box!" Benny suggested.

I walked over to the two identical sacks and lifted each one to determine which was the heaviest. I removed the metal box and handed it to my father.

Father examined the lock, and used the butt of his pistol and a nail he found to knock the lock in.

"Before I open it, what do you guess is in here?" he asked.

"Candy!" shouted Hanna.

"Money!" shouted Benny

"Sardines!" I shouted.

"Hmm, my guess is...frogs and leeches!" joked my father.

He slowly opened the lid and peeked inside the box. Inside were hundreds of tiny folded white envelopes.

"I know what these are," he stated. He picked up an envelope at random. It had some scribbling on it with some numbers. As he unfolded it, he saw that it contained a clear round polished crystal the size of a large blueberry.

"Diamonds!" my father exclaimed.

"How much are they worth?" Benny asked

"A fortune!" my father rejoiced. "When we get to America, we will open up a new watch store-- maybe in New York City. Our new name will be Imperial Watch and Diamond! And Benny, you will be a full partner! No more killing poor defenseless animals for you! We are all going into the jewelry business. Is that okay with you Benny!?"

Benny nodded. He was happy to be included in the business. After all, he was part of our family now.

"Everyone to bed! We have a busy day tomorrow," my father ordered.

We were glad that we were now safe, but there was a looming depression that affected us all. No matter how hard we tried, we could not feel happiness-- just emptiness. How could we? We lost more than anyone could ever imagine: Our families were senselessly murdered by Nazi animals. Our lives will never be the same again. I ask myself: Why did we survive while so many others didn't? It still feels like a nightmare to me that I hope to God I'll wake up from. But I never did.

Benny and I retired to our adjoining room, and Papa kept Hanna with him.

As my father tucked her in the bed, she asked again, "Papa, where is Mama?"

***

We awoke early the next morning and had breakfast in the hotel. My father suggested we split up on our way to the bus stop, since there might be either police or Germans looking for us.

They could have figured out that the SS officers had been poisoned by us. But did anyone really care that we killed a bunch of scum Nazis? Probably not likely.

We split up. I walked with Benny on one side of the street and Hanna rode on my father's shoulders on the other side. It didn't take long for us to arrive at the bus stop, but there was a long line of people waiting. When the bus finally arrived, everyone tried to squeeze on.

We were the last ones to make it on before the driver forced the door closed.

"How far to Stockholm?" father asked in Polish. The driver did not understand until my father pointed at the man's watch and then out the front window.

The driver held up two fingers. We supposed he meant two hours. The bus clanked along the hilly and windy roads stopping in small towns to drop off and pick up passengers.

After what seemingly took forever, we finally arrived in Stockholm.

It was the largest city I had ever seen. But regardless, we never really felt safe. We walked around a bit and stopped at a restaurant for lunch.

Miraculously the waitress spoke Polish.

Father asked the woman if there was a synagogue nearby.

She told him there was a great synagogue several blocks up the street near a large park. My father left her a hefty tip and we walked about a quarter kilometer to the park. Hanna was on my father's or Benny's shoulders, as usual.

It seemed odd to us, that people were freely walking and talking. They played with their children at the playground, seemingly without a care in the world. No Gestapo, no killing, no death camps. While across the sea there was a dark ominous storm raging on.

We continued walking until we found the synagogue.

The brick building was magnificent. Grander than any others we had ever seen. We walked up the steps and saw large Stars of David inlaid in the large wooden doors.

As we entered the building, the smell of old paper filled the air. There were five pentagonal shaped doors leading into the sanctuary. My father quietly pushed the center door open and we went in. Dark square columns braced the upper-level balcony, where the women would sit. There were rows upon rows of empty wooden benches that seemed to be awaiting their congregants to return for services. I thought sadly of the thousands of synagogue benches throughout Europe, whose congregations would never return. They would remain barren forever.

We walked down the aisle towards the podium. Behind it was the grand ark, which housed the sacred Torahs.

The ark was magnificent, with its carved wood and inlays of Biblical events. It was powerful. As we stood before it, my father began to weep. Benny too was trying to hold his tears back, sniffling and wiping his eyes. I was just standing there numb.

My father carefully opened the large wooden doors revealing several large ornate torahs inside. Each was sheathed in blue velvet and adorned with bright silver breastplates and dangling ornamental crowns.

"Lord" my father spoke softly, gazing into the ark. "My little girl Hanna has a question for you. She would like to know where her mother is. I don't know how to tell her. I was hoping that maybe you can explain it to her yourself.

"But please be gentle, Lord. She has a tiny little child's heart and it can be broken easily. I also want to let you know your people are crying for help. The Germans are slaughtering all the Jews in Europe. They are murdering innocent men, women and children. Yes, you heard me right, Lord-- children. Your people are praying for you with all their might to stop it.

"Who are we to understand your methods? We are nothing but beggars in life, always asking you for favors. But this is different. Why have you turned your back on us? We have not turned our backs on you, Lord. Can't you hear your children's desperate cries for help!!

"I only beg of you to now to turn back to us and destroy this wicked evil that has been bestowed upon us! Please God!!" pleaded my father.

We stood there silently for some time, mourning not only the death of our families. But for the death of every man, woman and child the Nazis murdered.

My father and Benny recited *Kadish*, the mourner's prayer while I held Hanna's hand. We stood in silence for a few minutes, waiting for a response, but it never came.

My father leaned into the ark and kissed the Torah. Benny did the same. They both looked at me, as I stood idle.

"I can't do it, Papa," I stated. "How can God allow this to happen to his people or any people? Little children torn away from their parents and viciously murdered. Babies tossed into trenches after being stabbed by Nazi bayonets! Whole families rounded up and slaughtered with no remorse. My grandparents murdered before our eyes. The atrocities are so overwhelming that I lost my faith!" I exclaimed.

My father nodded. He understood. And he turned me to face him, and he placed his hands on my shoulders and spoke to me intently, "You know, Koby. Someone was watching out for us, or we never would have made it this far."

"Yes Papa, but maybe we were just lucky," I replied.

"Maybe you are right that luck had something to do with our survival, but luck doesn't just happen, luck comes from somewhere, and I believe it came from God," my father stated.

I made a silly face and shrugged my shoulders in a manner that I thought "Maybe you are right" but I was still not convinced.

As we turned away from the ark, we noticed an old man standing by the podium behind us.

"Don't be alarmed," he said. "I am Rabbi Mordechai Erenpris. You must be 'The Watchmaker.'"

My father nodded.

The rabbi smiled and then embraced us.

"We heard of you and your children from the shortwave radio news. You are heroes, you know. Word has spread all over Europe and America about the Watchmaker and his three children. How they inflicted serious carnage to Hitler's regime," he raved.

"I listened to what you said about abandoning God boy. Don't you understand, you were chosen by God to avenge our people and give them hope and the strength to fight back! For every Nazi you destroyed, you helped save lives! Not only Jews, but Catholics, Gypsies and others who are being slaughtered. It's not only our people they are killing! As Moses was chosen by God to rescue the Jews from Egypt, you four were chosen for a different reason," he stated.

I nodded my head with respect to the rabbi and slowly returned to the ark. I forced myself to take hold of a Torah with my two fists and then I felt a powerful surge tingling in my hands.

The "ticking" in my brain began to sound as the force became more intense and traveled up my arms. My whole body was tingling and energizing as my grip tightened. I felt the awesome power of God as it pulsed through my body!

I leaned into the ark and placed my lips on the Torah, absorbing as much of its energy as I could.

Tears of sorrow filled my eyes as the waves of pent up emotion let go. I missed my mother and grandparents so much. I don't think I'll ever understand why this happened, nor will I ever forget. But I felt empowered.

Then the "ticking" abruptly stopped.

I turned and walked back to the rabbi, somehow feeling much differently.

"I'm sorry. I was wrong," I said.

***

My father then asked the rabbi for assistance, "We need to get to the American Embassy. Do you know where it is?"

The rabbi thought for a moment and held up his finger.

"Yes, I know! I will have my granddaughter bring you there," he said.

He disappeared for a moment and returned with a beautiful teenage girl.

She instantly walked over to Hanna and started to talk with her.

"Hi. My name is Sonya. What's your name?" she asked.

"Hanna," my sister shyly replied.

Benny couldn't take his eyes off her! For the first time ever, he was at a loss for words!

"Um...um...my name is Ben, Ben-yamin," he managed to stammer out!

My father and I chuckled as we watched him swoon over the girl. She was very pretty. It was rare for us to see a blue-eyed blonde Jewish girl. She even spoke our language. "Benyamin, where are you from?" she asked.

"Okay! Enough chattering!" her grandfather shouted. "Sonya, take them to the American Embassy and come right back."

We followed her out to the street and we walked through the park. She held Hanna's hand. And Benny was right beside her, relentlessly fixated on her.

He was trying to drum up conversation, but all he knew to converse about was how to slaughter animals, and it was obvious that it was disgusting to her!

Unfortunately for Sonya, once Benny got going he couldn't be shut up!

"There is the embassy, up there. You can see the American flags flying," she said.

As we approached the building, Benny began to panic. He never met a girl like Sonya before. If there was such a thing as love at first sight, this was it. He didn't want to say goodbye to her.

The steps up to the embassy were wide and tall. There were six heavily armed American soldiers dressed in pressed formal uniforms. Each was positioned at a specific place on the steps. A tall and muscular Sergeant stood at the base of the steps. His attire was slightly different than the other soldiers. He had an American cowboy hat on his head, and wore a pair of cowboy guns in holsters on his hips. They were fancy silver Colt Peacemaker six-shooters with ivory handles! Much like the ones we had seen Texas rangers carry in the western cowboy movies I saw in the cinema.

Sonya approached the Sergeant and spoke to him in English. She told him that we had important top-secret files that we obtained from the Germans, and we were seeking asylum. She also added that we would need a Polish- speaking interpreter.

The Sergeant, who had a heavy American southern accent, replied, "Y'all can go up, but I have to check your backpacks first."

As he searched, he removed the German pistol. But he didn't find Benny's *chalaf*, which Benny kept tied on his back, hidden under his shirt.

The sergeant was curious about the Nazi uniforms Benny had kept in his sack.

"Oh boy! If you side busters ever got caught by the krauts they would have strung y'all up like cattle rustlers for being spies," he remarked.

My father asked Sonya to translate.

"Something about breaking cows and making pies? I cannot understand this type of English!" she responded.

"Aw'll right, y'all ken go on up," stated the Sergeant.

"What kind of English do you speak sir? I cannot understand you so well?" said Sonya.

"The real English, Ma'am, I speak Texan!" he bragged.

He directed us up the steps, but Sonya said she couldn't go any further.

Benny began to look depressed and stared down at the ground. My father noticed an outside café across the street.

"Hey Ben Ben-yamin" my father chuckled, exaggerating the pronunciation of the name. "Why don't you take Sonya across the street and have some dessert together."

He handed Benny a fistful of money. Benny wasted no time! He grabbed Sonya's hand and they rushed to the cafe, laughing and pushing each other in jest as they crossed the street!

They sat down at an outside table next to the sidewalk. I could see that Benny-- for the first time-- was having fun.

My father motioned to the Sergeant that Benny would be joining us shortly. We labored up the long set of steps passing American soldiers along the way.

The main entrance door was opened for us by a soldier. In the reception area we were greeted by a woman dressed in a military uniform. She called for a translator and we were taken upstairs into an office. We sat on large leather armchairs with our backs to the windows as we waited for the translator.

The room overlooked the square. When I looked over my shoulder, I could see Benny holding

Sonya's hand on the table as they waited for their food.

A short man wearing a suit entered the room and offered Hanna and me some hard candy. He motioned to us that a translator would be here shortly and that he was the Ambassador.

As we sat and waited, we continued to spy on Benny.

Hanna and I thought it was funny, watching Benny schmooze with Sonya!

The translator finally entered the room and we directed our attention to her. My father gave them the documents we acquired and began telling them our story.

As Benny and Sonya enjoyed their desserts, an ominous German staff car slowly rolled up the street, stopping a short distance from the embassy. There were three German SS officers and a bloodied man hunched over and restrained in the back seat.

They sat there watching, when one of the officers suddenly noticed Benny at the café!

The three German officers quickly got out of the car and surrounded Benny and Sonya at their table.

They discreetly held their pistols under their hats. But the guns were trained on the couple.

Instantly, Benny recognised one of the men!

"Fancy meeting you here, Wolfie," he smirked.

"Shut up punk! Where is the rest of your Jew Screw?" Wolfie exclaimed.

"You told me to shut up. How am I supposed to answer you?" Benny replied.

Wolfie slapped him hard, but Benny didn't flinch.

"What happened to your neck Wolfie? It looks like that chop I gave you is going to leave a nasty scar!" Benny jeered. Wolfie cocked his pistol and aimed it at him. "You're too late Wolfgang, they are already inside the American Embassy.

Don't go over there though.

"Do you see that big American Sergeant wearing the cowboy hat, on the steps over there? He might mistake you for a cockroach and step on you!" Benny smirked.

"Get up, both of you!" Wolfie ordered.

Sonya was petrified and clung tightly to Benny's arm. They slowly stood up. Benny moved in front of her, shielding her.

"You can let her go. She is a Swedish citizen and is not involved," stated Benny.

Wolfie noticed a small golden Star of David on a chain around her neck.

He reached for it, but Benny instinctively grabbed a sharp pointed knife from the table and stabbed it into Wolfie's hand!

"Don't you touch her, you filthy piece of shit!" Benny shouted.

His men restrained Benny, as Wolfie pulled the knife out of his hand and threw it on the table.

"Take her too. She is a Jew," he ordered his men. He wrapped a handkerchief around his bleeding hand, biding his time for when he would have Benny all to himself. The officers began shoving them towards their staff car with their pistols.

Benny suddenly began fighting with the men! He shouted at Sonya to run away! She was too afraid; she didn't want to leave him! Then they hit Benny on the head with the butt of a pistol, knocking him semi unconscious. They began dragging the pair toward their staff car!

Meanwhile upstairs in the embassy, my father left the room to go to the bathroom. The translator offered us more candy. As we sat there sucking away on our pops, I glanced over my shoulder to see what Benny was up to.

I was stunned when I saw the Gestapo surrounding him and Sonya!

At once I jumped out of my seat and burst out the door! Running as fast as I could, I bolted down the steps, past the reception area, and out the front door! In my hast, I crashed into the Sergeant! I grabbed him by the arm with all my strength and pulled him into the street!

"Come, Texas! Nazis! Nazis!" I shouted, pointing to the cafe. By now, the three SS officers were forcibly dragging Benny and Sonya to their vehicle.

We raced diagonally across the street, and the other American soldiers quickly followed! They confronted the Germans, with their rifles aimed at them.

"Let them go, Krauts!" the Sergeant ordered.

"You are out of your jurisdiction, Sergeant!" Wolfie stated.

"So are you, Adolf. Now let 'em go!" the Sergeant ordered.

As I stood there, I noticed something on Wolfie's wrist as he pointed his gun at Benny. It was my precious gift, made by my grandfather. It was my golden watch!

"I think we have a standoff here, Sergeant," Wolfie continued. "If you shoot at us, we will kill the boy and girl." The Germans still had their pistols pointed at them.

"You drop *your* weapons," Wolfie ordered the Americans.

Acting as if he was distressed, the Sergeant dropped his rifle to the ground. He ordered his men to do the same.

Whereupon, Wofie began to laugh.

"Hah, hah, you stupid Americans. No wonder you will never win the war. You're too stupid! Now we are going to kill you too, as well as these dirty Jews!" he roared.

Both of Wolfie's German henchmen now aimed their weapons at the American soldiers.

But the Sergeant stated, "I'm gonna give you krauts a second chance to change your mind and let the young uns go! And I'm warn'in ya'll, as a bonafide Texas ranger, I have you out gunned!"

"Thank you, Sergeant, but I don't think you are in a position to give second chances! And it's not nice to make threats to your 'Superior officers' and you certainly don't have us out gunned!" chuckled Wolfie.

The other SS officers began laughing at Wolfie's remark.

I stood there petrified. Oddly, the American soldiers seemed relaxed and confident. One of them smiled at us and pretended to stretch and yawn. Another one played with a match stick in his mouth and winked at me. The others just stood there with their arms crossed and rolled their eyes as if they had something better to do.

They didn't seem concerned at all, that we were all about to die.

"Crazy Americans! These men are brave!" I thought.

"Aw'll right Major Kraut, don't say I didn't warn ya!"

The Germans smugly aimed their pistols at us! Wolfie kept his gun trained on Benny and Sonya, as they clung to each other tightly.

"Don't worry Benny, I have bigger plans for you and your Jew girlfriend later," chuckled Wolfie. "Kill them!" ordered Wolfie.

Once again the "ticking" in my head began! Tick... In that split second, the Sergeant instantly drew one of his fancy six-shooter pistols! He fanned it's hammer over and over with his left hand, as he aimed with his right!

Before anyone could react, he shot the two SS officers directly in the center of their foreheads, and they dropped completely dead to the street! In that same split second he shot the pistol out of Wolfie's hand! And lastly he put two bullets into his groin!

It all happened so fast! We had never seen anything like it!! He twirled his gun back and forth several times, then dropped it coolly back in its holster. He smiled at me and gave a big Texas wink!

"That's how we take care of bad hombres in Texas, kid!" he boasted.

"Okay, Sergeant, you had your fun. We need to get everyone back to the embassy before more krauts show up," one of the Americans warned.

Benny whispered something to Sonya. Then she told the Sergeant that the boys had something to do and would be back to the embassy in a short time.

I rushed over to the Sergeant and hugged him! "Thank you! Thank you, Texas!" I exclaimed.

"One riot, one ranger, kid," he replied with a smile. He strutted over to Wolfie, who was buckled over and in pain.

"Ouch, that musta hurt Major! You should never have messed with a Texas ranger!" he coolly remarked and tipped his cowboy hat.

"Boys you git your butts over to the embassy lickity split, ya hear!" he ordered.

Wolfie clutched his bleeding groin, as Benny quickly lunged at him from behind. He began to choke him with his arm, dragging him backwards into an alley, and I followed.

"Sonya, keep watch. Look out for anymore Germans or the police," Benny ordered. He didn't want her to witness what we were going to do to him.

Wolfie was bleeding badly. I began viciously kicking and punching him as he had done to my father the night they took us. I reached down to his hand and removed my golden watch from his wrist. It was covered in his blood, but I didn't care. I put it on. Though it hung loosely on my wrist.

"How does it look on *me* you Nazi piece of shit!?" I shouted.

"Please let me go. I need a doctor!" Wolfie begged.

"Oh, so now you want to talk to us? Benny, let him go. He needs a doctor," I said facetiously.

"It's payback time!" Benny shouted into his ear.

I picked up an old crusty brick that was lying on the ground and smashed it into Wolfie's ugly Nazi face as hard as I could! It made a "thud" sound. "This is for my grandparents and my mother," I raged as I struck him violently over and over again with the brick!

He wailed as blood poured from his shattered face, and he spit out several broken teeth.

I pulled off his coat and ripped his shirt off. "I want to see that ugly swastika you have tattooed under your armpit," I scorned.

Benny reached behind his neck and drew out his *chalaf*, as he held Wolfie firmly in a chokehold.

"Oh, there it is," I said, "but I want to see it up close. Benny, can you get me a closer look at Wolfie's Nazi tattoo?"

Benny took his blade and carved off a large chunk of flesh from under the tattoo and let it fall to the ground! Wolfie screamed out in pain! I picked up the flesh from the dirt and studied it.

"This little ugly thing makes you feel like a big man, even though you were always a good for nothing loser. Since you love this swastika so much I think you should choke on it!" I jeered.

I shoved the piece of filthy flesh into his bloody mouth and held my hand over it as he struggled to spit it out!

"What's the matter? It doesn't taste so good now does it?" I exclaimed.

"Please stop. I am begging you! I don't want to die!" mumbled Wolfie.

"Benny, are we still waiting for the doctor?" I joked.

"Okay Wolfie, I know you were afraid my Papa was going to circumcise you when you worked for us. Maybe his hand was a little shaky! But I have good news. Benny is going to circumcise you now. He is really good with a knife!" and then I brutally drove my knee to his bleeding groin and he screamed again.

Benny pulled back Wolfie's blond hair and pressed his blade against the flesh of his neck, and on the wound he had left. He began ever so slowly cutting through the skin of Wolfie's neck, guiding his blade around the curvature of his throat, being careful not to cut too deeply in order to draw out Wolfie's execution.

"Please, I beg you to stop!" Wolfie cried.

"So you want us to show you compassion?" Benny whispered. "How much compassion did you show our people?"

"It wasn't my fault! I was only following orders!" he cried.

"Oh Benny, let him go. He was 'just following his orders,'" I said sarcastically. "On second thought, follow *this* order, Benny," I continued.

I put my middle and pointer finger together and ran them across my throat--just as Wolfie had done to Benny the first day at the shop.

Wolfie's eyes became wild as Benny pressed his blade firmly against the bloody gaping skin of his throat and pulled his blade across in one long slow stroke, slicing completely through his throat!

Benny held him tightly, as his body flailed about, and he was struggling to die.

"I find you guilty for crimes against humanity, you will burn in hell with the rest of your Nazi scum," whispered Benny.

He released him into the gutter and wiped his blade on Wolfie's uniform.

My father had just arrived at the scene.

"Are you boys alright!" he exclaimed.

"Look, Papa. I got my watch back!" I said with delight.

My father gazed at the watch and then at the blood-drenched dead body. He recognized Wolfie's half amputated head.

"How did he know where to find us?" he questioned.

We shrugged our shoulders. As we turned back to the embassy, my father noticed the badly beaten man, bound in the back of the staff car. He realized it was Fritz, our pilot!

"I'm sorry, Watchmaker. They found me on the beach and tortured me to tell them where you were going," he moaned.

"There is another man who knows...." He tried to tell us, but then he passed out.

My father released Fritz's restraints and pulled him from the car. Father and Benny carried him into the embassy, as Sonya and I followed.

The Sergeant ordered a few soldiers and a medic to take him. He was barely breathing, but alive.

Sonya reported that this German pilot helped us escape and that he needed asylum.

"Giddy up, boys!" the Texan shouted to them.

Sonya and Benny embraced on the steps of the embassy. She cried and said she didn't want to leave him.

Benny silently looked to my father for help. How could they somehow stay together?

"Sonya, your grandfather and parents must be worried that you have not returned," my father said. But Sonia had a surprising confession.

"I am not from here. I am from Denmark, sir. My parents sent me to Sweden so I would be safe before the Germans invaded our country.

"My grandfather is actually no relation to me at all, but he was a dear friend to our rabbi in Denmark. He took me in as a favor to keep me safe from the Germans. I have not heard from my parents in over six months. I was told that they were taken away and thrown off a boat into the sea!" she cried.

"Come, let's all go into the embassy and see how we can work this out," my father said.

We walked up the stairs and returned to the room we were in.

Benny and I were covered in blood. Hanna was still sitting in her chair with the female translator by her side and the Ambassador on the other. She was still eating candy.

The translator was taken aback when she saw Benny and me covered in blood. She asked what happened. I responded that someone we knew had gotten a bloody nose and that he was waiting for a doctor to come.

The Ambassador rose. He had been looking through the documents we brought in. He informed us that some of the maps were locations of death camps all over Europe. They would be useful for Allied bombers to take out the trains and help liberate the people. Another file contained top-secret plans of a German attack on the American allies.

There were also many documents and pictures of Nazi officers and collaborators that played part in the regime.

The Ambassador told us we had done the American Army a great service by obtaining these files. A special military plane would take us to Washington, D.C., where we could tell our story to the war department. He also told us that the United States government would be granting us asylum! We were going to become citizens of the USA!

Benny interrupted the translator and asked about Sonia.

"If her family can produce her paperwork, she can go for a temporary visit, but she will have to return before her visa expires," the Ambassador stated.

"A temporary visit! That's not good enough!" cried Benny.

The Ambassador thought for a moment.

"How long have you known each other?" he asked.

"They just met this morning at the synagogue," replied my father.

The Ambassador rubbed his face and shook his head in anguish.

"Okay, how old are you kids?" he questioned.

"I'm sixteen," replied Sonya

"I'm fifteen, but I will turn sixteen in 8 days!" declared Benny

The ambassador again rubbed his face and hair, as if to consider the options.

"There is only one-way Sonia can go with you permanently to America, Benny. You have to marry her!" stated the Ambassador.

Benny smiled and looked into Sonya's eyes. "Sonya, will you marry me?" he quickly asked.

My father and I stood there in shock as the words echoed in the room.

Everyone's attention turned toward Sonia, as we awaited her response. We expected her to say no.

"*Yes*, I will marry you Ben, Ben---yamin!" she exclaimed.

My father and I looked at each other, made silly faces and shrugged our shoulders.

The Ambassador said he would invite the rabbi over to perform the ceremony when they were ready.

"I'll have one of the armed soldiers and the translator escort her back to her grandfather to explain what's going on," he added.

"Sir, the rabbi she is living with is not really her grandfather, but a kind man who took her in to hide her in Sweden from the Germans," said my father.

"Nevertheless he is the girl's guardian," stated the Ambassador.

He called his assistant on his telephone. Shortly after, a soldier arrived to escort the translator and Sonya back to the synagogue.

Benny and Sonya hugged and kissed each other as they parted. It was the happiest I had ever seen him, and the first time I had ever seen him kiss a girl!

Benny peered out the window and watched Sonya as she walked down the embassy's steps and left. He noticed the police were on the scene, removing the dead bodies. He could see the table where he had been sitting with Sonya at the café. Then he noticed his rucksack was still sitting there, under the table.

"Kobie! I left my rucksack at the café! I'll be right back!" he exclaimed. He raced out the door and past the soldiers on the steps, and he dashed across the street to the café. Luckily he was able to retrieve his sack and he joyfully slung it over his shoulder. As he was about to head back to the embassy he smiled as he thought of the happiness Sonya had brought to him, after he believed he could never be happy again.

As he stepped out of the cafe, a stranger lunged and stabbed him in the back with a large hunting knife! The man ripped the bag off Benny's shoulder and ran off with it!

As Benny collapsed he took note of his assaulter. It was the fisherman!

As it turned out, he had stumbled on Wolfie and his henchmen as they were torturing Fritz, the pilot. He must have overheard Fritz state something about the "American Embassy." The fisherman was still chasing after the treasure of gold coins. He ran off with Benny's sack, but in fact it contained only the uniforms and some files. Blood was pouring from Benny's wound and he began to feel his life leaving his body. He began coughing up blood and struggled to breath, then faintly he heard gunfire coming from the American soldiers' guns. Sadly, he closed his eyes, and whispered, "Sonya...".

Chapter Seven

My father had a cousin in Queens, New York, who offered to help us get situated in America. A year had passed, and we had opened the Imperial Watch and Diamond shop in the jewelry district of Manhattan.

The store was successful, and we hung our old doorbell from our shop in Poland onto our new door in Manhattan. I turned thirteen, and tomorrow, on the Sabbath, I am reciting my *Bar Mitzvah*. We are having a small ceremony in our new synagogue. The rabbi informed me that I was going to become a man tomorrow. But I knew that after all that I had been through, I am a man already.

It was Friday afternoon, and we were preparing to close our shop for the Sabbath. I asked my father if I could now wear the precious watch my grandfather made for me. I desperately wanted to have my special watch and finally see the message my grandfather had written inside on the back of the case.

"Okay, Kobie, I think your grandfather would be proud if you would wear this during your *Bar Mitzvah* tomorrow. I'll open it for you," he said.

He took the watch from the vault and removed the back plate with a special tool, exposing the inner gears and the inside of the back plate.

There was a short inscription engraved on the plate which read:

"Jacob, my love for you is as great as the stars that streak across the skies. I will always be with you, *Zaydee*"

I began to weep as I thought about the night at the airfield, and the SS officers were about to kill us. When I looked up into the sky, and I saw that bright shooting star "How could something so beautiful show up now?" I had reluctantly wondered that night.

That was a message: It was from my grandfather. He was watching over me.

In this sacred moment, the front door abruptly swung open, knocking the bell off the door and creating a crashing sound as it hit the floor. I wiped away my tears and handed the watch back to my father.

I peeked out from the workshop and I saw a young couple with their backs to me. They were laughing and pushing each other as they competed to pick up the bell from the floor and place it back on the door. After all the sorrow we had endured, it was good to hear laughter.

"Hey! 'Short and Sharp!'" I shouted.

Benny and Sonia happily turned to me and smiled.

"All of them, Kobie...All of them!" replied Benny.

Short and Sharp!

COMING SOON

The Watchmaker Part II
"The Chosen"

Ten years had passed, and the Watchmaker and his family were now settled into their thriving business in the jewelry district of Manhattan. Despite their emotional hardships, they manage to try to move on from the horrors of the Holocaust. Until one day a mysterious stranger appears in their shop. He was there to tell them his heinous story of what had happened to his wife and two little boys by the hands of a Nazi demon. He had devoted what was left of his empty life, searching for the scum that perpetrated the sadistic murder of his family. Now he finally had knowledge of his whereabouts. In his mind, there was only one family that could help him seek justice and retribution. He was there to ask the Watchmaker, Kobie and Benny to help him hunt down and destroy one of the most diabolical Nazi butchers of all time.